THE
GREAT
REVOLT

THE
GREAT
REVOLT

PAUL DOWSWELL

BLOOMSBURY EDUCATION
LONDON   OXFORD   NEW YORK   NEW DELHI   SYDNEY

BLOOMSBURY EDUCATION
Bloomsbury Publishing Plc
50 Bedford Square, London, WC1B 3DP, UK

BLOOMSBURY, BLOOMSBURY EDUCATION and the Diana logo are trademarks of
Bloomsbury Publishing Plc

First published in Great Britain in 2020 by Bloomsbury Publishing Plc

A catalogue record for this book is available from the British Library

ISBN: PB: 978-1-4729-6842-5; ePDF: 978-1-4729-6841-8; ePub: 978-1-4729-6840-1

2 4 6 8 10 9 7 5 3 1

Typeset by Newgen KnowledgeWorks Pvt. Ltd., Chennai, India
Printed and bound by CPI Group (UK) Ltd, Croydon CR0 4YY

All papers used by Bloomsbury Publishing Plc are natural, recyclable products from wood
grown in well managed forests. The manufacturing processes conform to the environmental
regulations of the country of origin

To find out more about our authors and books visit www.bloomsbury.com
and sign up for our newsletters

CHAPTER ONE

June 1, 1381

Matilda Rolfe shivered in her woollen blankets and watched the lightning flash in the reflections of the puddles on the mud floor of her hut. Her straw mattress was still slightly damp from the last time they'd had a storm, and she had moved her bedding to the driest part of the hut, where the thatched roof was most secure. Outside the rain poured down in sheets and the trees behind the house rattled and rustled in the fierce wind. The smell of wet cob – that mixture of straw, soil and animal droppings that made up the walls – lodged in her nostrils.

Matilda had put on all her clothes and she was still cold. Last year they had had two old dogs and they loved to snuggle up with her at night and keep her warm. But Sturdy and Holdfast had both died over the winter. When a neighbour's dog had had a litter in the spring Matilda had asked if they could have a couple, but her father, Thomas, had told her sadly they could not afford to feed them. Maybe next year they would have dogs again.

Earlier in the night, Thomas had given her his spare blanket. She had been half awake when he had draped it over her, whispering, 'You keep warm, Tilda,' and now she could hear him snoring away behind the wicker partition on the other side of the hut. She felt a twinge of guilt, letting him give her that blanket, but he was a tough old boar and the cold and stormy night was not preventing him from sleeping.

Lightning flashed again, illuminating the outlines of the glassless windows and their wooden baffles, and lighting up those puddles. The water on the floor was not creeping any closer. Reassured that she was not in danger of waking under a stream of rainwater, Tilda began to drift off to sleep. Another great gust of wind shook the hut and she started awake again, wondering why God was so angry to visit them with a storm like this. Was it their sinful ways? She and Thomas lived a blameless life, working for the lord of the manor in his fields, and tending to their own needs on the little strip of land he let them farm.

People called them serfs, or villeins, and they were tied to their lord and their village. Everyone else around them was the same. Everyone went to church and there was no whiff of witchcraft among the humble folk of Aylesford village. So maybe it was their betters who had aroused the wrath of God?

Three months ago an extraordinary man of God had visited the village and preached to them all on the green. John Ball had said something she had not been able to forget:

When Adam delved and Eve span,
Who was then the gentleman?

She loved that – she and her father delved the land – turning and tending to the soil in the fields. And Tilda's mother, Mary, had been a spinner of flax before she died giving birth to a stillborn little sister. Tilda could picture her mother now, sitting by the fire with her wheel and spindle. And what Ball said was true. The world God created in the Garden of Eden wasn't the world they lived in. They were slaves to the lords and ladies who treated common people like them with contempt. Their local lord, William Laybourne, was hated by most of the villagers she knew – apart from her neighbours, Walter and Elspeth Cooper, who no one trusted.

A few days after he had visited the village, John Ball had been arrested. They heard he was held in Maidstone Gaol. Tilda felt indignant about that. She was convinced that what he'd said was plainly true. Not that her father agreed with her. He thought they ought to keep their heads down and tug their forelocks to the lord of the manor, and anyone else who served the king. Tilda held her tongue. She loved her father and did not want to make him angry. He said talk like that was rebellious, traitorous even. And besides, there were terrible punishments for those who spoke against the rulers of the land.

Tilda had seen what happened to traitors when she was barely ten years old. Four years earlier, two men from Aylesford were said to have been spying for the French. And the way they were dealt with had made Tilda's stomach churn in leaden fear. The wretches were dragged through the main street by a horse, then taken to the scaffold and hanged until near death. Then their breeches were pulled down and they were castrated. That was barely the start of it. The hangman had bought some hideous spooling device and cut the men in the innards, pulling out their guts from their insides. They both died sometime during that hideous ordeal and even in death their indignity was not yet over. Their lifeless bodies were beheaded, and then cut into four pieces. The whole village had been made to watch this disgusting spectacle. Four years on, the memory of it, and the screams of the victims, still haunted her. She wondered whether they would do that to a girl like her, or whether it was just men who had to endure such dreadful tribulations.

*

Sometime during the night the storm subsided and Tilda slept. She woke to see her father standing over her.

'It's daybreak, my dearing,' he said softly. 'Here's some porridge to start your day.' A wooden bowl and a small jug of milk lay by the side of her mattress.

'What a night,' said Tilda, gathering her curly thatch of black hair to tie behind her head with a leather thong. The air was chilly and she was reluctant to stir from the meagre warmth of her bed.

'Coopers lost half their roof,' said Thomas, trying to sound nonchalant about it. But Tilda could tell he was pleased.

'Ours just about stayed put. Only a bit of water come through,' said Tilda, spooning in a mouthful of warming porridge.

Thomas shook his head. 'This old hut's only got another year in it, before it rots around us. We need to talk to Laybourne about finding somewhere else to live.'

Tilda frowned. 'He'll probably just tell us we can move in with the pigs in the sty,' she said. Then she smiled. 'Actually, they live in a little stone shelter with a nice timber roof, so they're better off than us!'

'Not seen a storm like this since I was a child,' said Thomas, anxious to change the subject. Tilda knew he didn't like her to be 'disrespectful'. But she couldn't help herself.

'We had one like that just before the plague arrived in the village,' Thomas went on. 'God has ways of warning his flock...' He trailed off, a look of bleak concern flashing across his face. Tilda felt a bolt of fear. She had heard enough tales about the plague to know it was the worst thing that could happen to her world.

Thomas changed his tune. 'Still, storm's passed now and the sun is shining,' he said. 'Look, here's Catherine.' A small red squirrel had appeared beside Tilda's bed. It quickly hopped on to her shoulder and she put down her bowl to fuss it. 'Don't let your breakfast go cold,' he said and got up to tend to his chores. As he left the room he said, 'We're harrowing the strip by Lord's Field this morning. Be sure to bring your sling.'

Tilda nodded. She resented having to work for the lord of the manor, especially for the tiny wage he paid them. There he was, swanning around in a hat beaded with pearls and a red velvet jacket, and the rest of them in rags, having to wear everything they owned to keep warm at night.

'It'll never do,' she said softly to Catherine, stroking the side of her head. 'One day, we shall leave this wretched life behind, and we'll take you with us, Your Highness.'

Catherine gave a long trill, the sort of noise she made when she was happy, and Tilda reached under her bed to give her a cob nut. She loved the way the squirrel stood upright and clasped food in its front paws to eat it. Tilda called her Catherine, a royal name, because she treated her like a princess.

'You, I don't mind looking after, you love me back,' she whispered. 'But Lord William Laybourne, I could do without helping him at all. And his stuck-up son...'

Breakfast done, Tilda and Thomas walked across the common to collect their horse, Brownie, and his harrow. The air was fresh and breezy and all around there was evidence of the damage the storm had wreaked, in fallen trees and fences, and battered buildings.

Tilda thought of her father's warning. 'Do you think the plague is coming back?' she asked.

Thomas looked uncertain. 'It's returned before, but never as bad as when I was a boy. That was horrible, Tilda. I hope you never see anything like that. People covered in swellings as large as eggs, oozing blood and pus. It makes me sick to think of it. And they died in a day. We lost over half the village in a few weeks.'

Tilda had heard these stories many times. She put an arm round him, nestling under his shoulder. 'But not you and Mum,' she said.

Thomas put his brave face on. 'Might not be plague that's coming,' he said. 'Might be something else. Who knows what God has in store for his flock.'

CHAPTER TWO

Brownie lived in a little wooden stable next to Lord's Wood and the biggest field on the estate. The harrow he would pull had been leaning against the stable but had fallen over in the storm. Thomas and Tilda picked it up together. The heavy wooden beams and great iron nails were certainly more than Tilda could pick up on her own.

'We shouldn't let that get too wet,' said Thomas. 'Wood'll go rotten and the nails'll rust. We should have put it inside yesterday afternoon.'

Lord Laybourne called from a distance. 'You, Rolfe. I want a word.'

'What's this about?' muttered Tilda.

'I can guess,' said Thomas, looking at the harrow.

But before the lord could get any closer, he was surrounded by several irate villagers. He looked distracted and his hand went instinctively to the hilt of his sword. Even from a distance Tilda could sense his disdain – he had the expression and manner of a man in the presence of a powerfully unpleasant smell. Maybe he was, thought Tilda with a smile. Some of the villeins still thought a hearty smell let the world know they were bursting with manly vigour. How such men thought this would make them attractive to women was beyond her understanding. She was grateful her father did not cling to that old-fashioned idea.

They walked forward, as angry words drifted towards them in the light wind. Laybourne was almost a head taller than the peasants around him, but he was a lean and wiry man, and probably no match for a thickset peasant intent on doing him harm. But the closer they got the more it became clear that the men who surrounded him were angry about something else and were expecting him to help them.

Eustace Fogg, who lived across the village from the Rolfes, was in a desperate state. 'You must help, my lord, I beg you. My brother, Peter of Larkfield, has been arrested.'

'I'm sure for good reason,' said Laybourne sharply.

'No, my lord, his daughter was assaulted by a tax collector.'

Laybourne's face remained impassive. 'The collectors have too much work to do, surely? They would not have time to assault the young women of the parish.'

Fogg tried to contain his anger. 'My lord, the collectors demanded a whole twelve pence from everyone in the village over the age of fifteen.'

'I know,' said Laybourne. He sounded weary. 'I was instructed by the county constable to levy such a charge. Those men work directly for me.'

'But my lord...' Fogg had gone red in the face with anger. 'This collector, he told Peter's daughter she would have to pay. She's only thirteen. The lecherous goat said he did not believe her and pulled up her gown to her chest. He made her naked for all the world to see...' The others around them stood silent in shock. Laybourne tried to arrange his face into an expression of concern. 'And this man leered at her and declared to her father that *he* was obviously a liar and *she* was obviously a fine young woman and old enough for sure to pay the tax.'

Laybourne shook his head and spoke firmly. Tilda thought his was a tone of voice an adult would use to speak to a stubborn child. 'The collectors are charged by the king to raise revenue for the crown. There is a war with France to be paid for. Money does not grow on a magic money tree. How would this man know your brother was not lying about his daughter's age?'

Fogg could sense he had no chance of winning this argument. He was clearly at a loss for what to say next.

Another man spoke for him. 'My lord, Peter Fogg was so enraged at the collector's lechery, he grabbed a shovel and split the man's head open.'

'And did the collector die of his wound?' asked Laybourne. This time, he sounded concerned.

The man nodded.

'Then Fogg will hang within a week.'

The pronouncement put an end to the meeting. Laybourne strode away, fixing Tilda and Thomas with a stern eye. 'You left the harrow out last night. If you do it again you will be fined a week's wages.'

Thomas lowered his eyes in shame. 'Yes, my lord. It was my fault.' Tilda had forgotten to do it. Her father was protecting her.

Laybourne's eye alighted on Tilda. He gave her a crooked smile. 'And how old are you, young woman? Is anyone going to be lifting your gown up to check on your age?'

Thomas stood before him, his meekness gone.

'My daughter is only fourteen, my lord,' he said firmly.

Laybourne shrugged. 'I won't tell you again about the harrow.' Then he turned around and sauntered back to the manor house with a slate roof, where the Rolfes both noticed there were four chimneys billowing smoke from fires to ward off the late spring chill.

*

Eustace Fogg looked like he had seen a ghost. 'I would have acted the same if that man had done that to my daughter.'

Thomas Rolfe put a hand on his shoulder. 'Who knows what a man will do in the heat of anger,' he said. 'I am sorry your brother is in such deep trouble.'

Fogg's voice hardened. 'Storm like last night always means trouble. Who knows what's coming our way?'

Alone now, Tilda and Thomas led Brownie out of his stable and let him graze on the thick grass. They walked the harrow clumsily out to the side of the field and prepared the leather harnesses. 'This one's only got a few more days in it,' said Tilda, holding up a worn length.

Thomas called Brownie over with a carrot he produced from his tunic. As the horse gobbled away, Tilda quickly attached his harness to the harrow. They were about to set off to till the field when another distraction overtook them. Hugh Godfrey, one of Laybourne's men, was hailing them.

'Rolfe, tax collectors will be here tomorrow,' he said. 'A shilling from everyone over fifteen.' He turned to Tilda and smiled. 'You should be all right,' he said kindly. 'You were baptised here weren't you? Ask them to check the parish records if they query your age.' Then he hared off, looking for other farm labourers to tell.

'We're paying for you, Tilda. I'm not having no grubby collector lifting up your gown.'

'Anyone who does that to me will have his nose broken,' said Tilda.

'Attacking a tax collector can have serious consequences, my dearing. You might even be accused of treason.'

Tilda was outraged. 'But it's a whole week's wages, Father. We have barely enough to eat. And almost no fuel for our fire.'

'We'll manage,' said Thomas. And that was the end of that discussion.

He left Tilda to her thoughts. She shrugged. A week's wages for an unexpected poll tax was something that made her angry but it wasn't going to kill them. If the storm was a warning, then surely God had something far worse than that up his sleeve.

*

That night, Tilda lay in her bed and pondered on the injustices of the world. This was their lot. Laybourne owned them, like he owned the buildings and the land in and around the village, and he could sell them like cattle. When she first discovered this, when her father had told her about it one evening, she had been outraged.

Funnily enough, Thomas didn't seem to mind. 'Tilda, my dearing, we get a place to live and we get land to work on and grow our food. What else can we do? We cannot read and write; we can only work the land. God has given us a good life. Or at least a life we can bear.'

'We can run away, Father,' she had said.

Thomas had smiled sadly. 'We haven't got much in this world have we, sweet Matilda?' he said, sweeping his arm about the sparse interior of their hut. 'But if we ran away we'd have absolutely nothing. We have friends around us, we're born to work the soil and we'll live and die as villeins. It's God's will. We can't go against it.'

Even as a twelve-year-old hearing this for the first time, Tilda felt a sense of burning injustice in her father's words. But she could see the sense in them too. What else could they do?

'But what about Uncle John?' she had said. Thomas had mentioned she had an uncle who lived in London. He had escaped from the village before she was born.

'Yes, he was lucky. He made use of his skill with wood. He became a carpenter and house-builder,' said Thomas. 'And it's true. If you can live in a city for a year and a day then you are free of the bond that ties you to the lord of the manor.'

'Why can't we do that, Father?' said Tilda.

Thomas just shook his head. He wasn't even angry. 'Because I like my village and I like my neighbours and I like the countryside. Big towns are places where everyone lives on top of everyone else, and there is pestilence, and you can't get the smell of dung out of your nostrils. Tilda, let's talk no more about this. The evils of the city are far greater than the evils of our servitude to Lord Laybourne.'

So Tilda never raised the subject again, but that did not stop her thinking about it. Sometimes she would fantasize about being a travelling performer – a juggler or an acrobat. She wondered if she could create an act using her skills with a slingshot – but she quickly realised that wasn't something that would enthral people in a street circus and get them to part with money. She wondered too about playing a musical instrument. From time to time, wandering minstrels had visited Aylesford and the sound they made always enchanted her. But she had no idea how much a hurdy-gurdy or a crumhorn cost and didn't have the first idea how she would go about learning to play such a thing. But people told her she had a good singing voice. Maybe she could use that?

The truth was, there was very little she could do that offered her a better life than the one that was mapped out before her. Even if she had been born a boy, the choices were still very limited. One older boy from the village, she remembered, had run away to Rochester to work on the fishing boats. That sounded better than what she had to look forward to here. But no one would allow a girl to become a fisherman – it was bad luck to have women on board a boat, she was told. Tilda hated all that. 'Women are the ruin of mankind,' she was always being told. They couldn't do a thing right in the eyes of some men. In church she had to listen to the story of Genesis and how Eve had tempted Adam with the apple.

Tilda had begun to doubt those stories and could see how they were useful in keeping the villeins in their place. But she dare not share her thoughts. It was too dangerous. Heretics would be sent to hell and Tilda did not want to burn in a lake of fire for all eternity. She didn't want her friends and neighbours to shun her either, and that's what would happen if she started to argue with their local priest on a Sunday morning.

Even if she did run away to Rochester, her job would be to wait for the men to return from the sea and then spend the day gutting fish. It was a dreary prospect. Mind you, although plenty drowned on fishing boats no one ever died gutting fish, unless they got into an argument with another fish-gutter that ended in a knife fight.

In her wilder fantasies, Tilda wished she could read and write. If she could do that, she thought, she would never be bored. The mother of her friend Cecily had been able to write. She worked in nearby Maidstone, keeping records for a local brewer who was related to Laybourne. That seemed like a nice life. They even had a book in their hut, a gift from the brewers to their valued employee. It was full of stories about faraway lands.

When Cecily and Tilda were young, they would sit as her mother read them fantastical tales of tribes who had faces on their chests rather than heads, and trees that produced live lambs rather than fruits and seeds. To Tilda, that brown leather-bound book seemed like the most valuable thing in the world, and sometimes Cecily's mother would let her hold it. And even though those squiggly lines and circles and curves were puzzling now, one day she would learn to read, she told herself.

Tilda missed Cecily. The family had moved to Maidstone with Laybourne's blessing. One Sunday, when she had an afternoon off, she would try to find her there.

CHAPTER THREE

The work was the same as it always was, the early morning still chill enough for Brownie's breath to stream like steam from his nostrils. But the breeze stayed gentle and the sky stayed blue and the summer would soon be here. Thomas led the horse as they harrowed the field, churning the soil ready for planting barley. Tilda followed on behind, carrying a bag full of stones and a slingshot. They were not planting yet, but she needed the practice and whenever a bird landed to investigate she would hurl a stone towards it.

Tilda did not like to kill the birds. They were hungry just as she was, and she prided herself on landing her stone just next to her target – enough to frighten it off but not harm it. Thomas hardly ever saw how good she had become – all this was going on behind him, after all – but she was always pleased when he praised her skill with that slingshot.

'You're as a good as a boy,' he would say.

'I'm better, Father,' she would reply.

The village boys often teased her about it, telling her such a talent was not ladylike. Tilda shrugged off such nonsense and was happy to thump any boy she felt was getting too cocky. Besides, they didn't complain when she used her skill to dislodge fruit high up in the boughs of an apple tree.

Mid-morning, she sensed Thomas and Brownie were tiring and waited patiently for her father to declare it was time for a rest. But her attention was drawn to the sound of an angry crowd approaching along the Larkfield road. Shielding her eyes from the bright sun, she squinted into the distance. Peter Fogg, she noticed with a frisson of alarm, was there at the head of the crowd, along with the village blacksmith and several burly farm labourers she recognised. Fogg called ahead, urging any Aylesford villagers within earshot to gather round.

Thomas looked on suspiciously. 'If Peter Fogg has escaped from prison, then he is an outlaw. If any of Laybourne's men see him, they would be entitled to slay him on the spot. And it would be our duty to do that too.'

Tilda clutched her father's arm. She could see the blacksmith carried a heavy hammer, and several of the farm labourers had their scythes and rakes with them. 'It'd take a brave man to tackle that lot,' she said.

The arrivals mustered on the village green and several score villagers hurried in from the fields to join them in a large circle. Peter Fogg stepped forward from the crowd and declared, 'I have been freed from prison by my friends.' He turned to bow his head. These men had taken the law into their own hands. Now they were just as guilty as he – felons who faced the hangman's noose. What was going on in the world? thought Tilda. What he said next was even more shocking.

'The king is led by flatterers and evil-doers at court,' Fogg declared. 'It is they who work us to the bone for a pittance and tax us so unjustly.' There was a half-hearted murmur of agreement from the villagers. What he said was undoubtedly true, but they all knew it was treason to say it. 'Take heart,' cried Fogg. 'News reaches us of other villagers rising up in Essex and Kent, and a great march to London to petition the king and demand justice for us all.'

This was extraordinary news, but Tilda could sense Thomas growing tense beside her. His usually ruddy face had gone almost white. 'We shall all be hanged as traitors,' he called out to the crowd.

It was not a popular opinion. The others looked on him with impatience.

'Rolfe, you're not like those Coopers – spying on your neighbours for the lord of the manor. Surely you can see the justice of our cause?' said Fogg.

'Fairness and decency has nothing to do with the world we live in, no matter what the church says,' said another man Tilda did not recognise. 'We have to take a stand.'

Thomas turned to speak to him. 'My friends and neighbours,' he said. 'You know I am no coward.' There was a general murmur of assent. Tilda looked at her father with pride. He had done so many things to help his neighbours – most recently driving away a mad dog with foaming jaws who was threatening a group of children. And last summer he had dived into the River Medway to rescue a woman who was drowning.

'But you all know the penalty for rebellion.' He turned to Tilda. 'I love my daughter. She has already lost her mother. I don't want her to see her father hanged. Or, God forbid, have her hang beside me.' He turned to the broad boughs of an oak tree on the side of the field. 'They will hang us along those branches. I know they would be cruel enough to do it.'

There was a low murmur from the crowd. Not of agreement, but not of hostility either. Maybe Thomas was winning them round and caution would win the day after all.

'Here comes Laybourne,' someone cried out, pointing in the direction of the manor house.

'And three of his overseers,' shouted another.

The crowd turned to look. In the distance they saw the lord approaching. But he looked hesitant.

'Show them you mean business,' said a voice in the crowd. Clearly no one was in the mood to listen to Thomas Rolfe. They began to shake their scythes and rakes and jeer with surprising venom. Lord Laybourne and his men turned on their heels and began to run back to the manor.

Thomas shook his head, but Tilda clutched his arm and said, 'If we can talk directly to the king we will make things better.'

'Tilda, my dearing, what do you know of kingship? These are mortal, dangerous words.'

The crowd around them were roused, emboldened by their little victory over Laybourne. They headed off in the direction of the village of Eccles, hoping to stir up more villeins with their talk of rebellion.

Tilda and Thomas returned to their field and continued with their work. Tilda still felt angry with her father, and not a word passed between them. But she was shrewd enough to know that this was not the right time to discuss it. She thought of the words from *Ecclesiastes*: 'A time to keep silent and a time to speak', which she has heard in church sermons from time to time. As they harrowed the field, she was lost in her own thoughts and another verse from *Ecclesiastes* popped into her head: 'And also that every man should eat and drink, and enjoy the good of all his labour, it is the gift of God'. She will mention this when they get round to discussing what they should do.

The sun sank lower in the sky, and just as the air began to cool on the fields, Lord Laybourne reappeared. He was accompanied by two of his retinue who carried swords. 'What was that calumny, Rolfe?' he demanded. 'I can't have a mob rampaging on my estate.'

'We were busy harrowing, your lordship,' said Thomas, his face set in a mask.

'But who were those villeins?' demanded Laybourne impatiently.

'From another village I suppose, I certainly didn't recognise any of them,' said Thomas.

'And where did they go?' asked one of Laybourne's men, as if speaking to a simple child.

Tilda pointed in a direction opposite to the one the crowd took. She said nothing.

'And where are the other villagers?' said Laybourne.

Thomas and Tilda looked blank.

With a weary sigh Laybourne turned and walked slowly back to the manor house.

*

There was a further interruption late that afternoon too. Hugh Godfrey had been right. The tax collectors did descend on the village.

'You, villein,' shouted a thickset young man on horseback. 'Where are the inhabitants of this village?'

Thomas eyed him with the same plain expression. 'Village never really recovered from the plague, sir. So it's just us here today.'

The young man dismounted as two soldiers rode up behind him. The soldiers stayed on their horses, silent and menacing. The fellow circled them slowly, trying to catch Tilda's eye. But she would not let him. Whenever he looked into her face she looked away.

The young man picked up a short stave resting against a stable wall and Thomas stepped forward. 'Do you mean us harm, sir?' he said, letting them know he would not be meek in the face of violence.

The young man gave him a smile that did not reach his eyes. He sauntered close to Tilda and lifted her long skirt above her shins. 'And how old is this young wench?' he said.

Tilda looked at him with contempt, anger boiling in her eyes. 'I am fourteen,' she said, daring him to disbelieve her. The young man swallowed and she could sense an excitement rising within him. 'You look older than fourteen to me,' he said, raising her skirt a little higher.

Thomas Rolfe stood boldly before him, causing him to step back. 'She is of age. I will pay the tax you have come to collect.'

The soldiers rode their horses closer and the young man gave Tilda a hefty thwack on her backside with the stave, causing her to stagger forward. 'I could have you punished for lying to an agent of the crown,' he said. 'But the day is nearly done. I will record your names and take your tax.'

Tilda was surprised to see her father had already brought the money with him. He took twelve pennies for each of them from a small bag at his waist and made sure the collector recorded their names. 'And what of your wife, peasant?' said the young man. 'Where might she be found?'

'She is in the churchyard, sir,' said Thomas boldly. 'I am sure the crown has not yet resorted to taxing the dead.'

The young man shrugged. Tilda could almost spot his brain whirring, trying to come up with a suitable witty reply. He failed and instead mounted his horse without another word, and the three of them trotted off towards Laybourne's manor house.

CHAPTER FOUR

Most of the villagers who had left with the rebels returned that night, their eyes wide with excitement. Tilda wanted to talk to them but was anxious not to upset her father. But that night over a supper of potage she did talk to him about what had happened that day.

'That money you gave them, we could have spent it on a repair for the roof,' said Tilda.

'We'll just have to do it ourselves,' said Thomas. Then he grew angry. 'I'm not having them humiliating you, Tilda. I know you're only fourteen but you look like a young woman now.'

Tilda bowed her head. She was not going to get into an argument about this. She knew Thomas should have told them to look in the parish records to check her age, but she suspected they would have ignored him. And she knew he was only trying to protect her.

His voice softened. 'Tilda, my dearing, I know this is not right. That's the third poll tax we've had in four years. It's plain unfairness, taxing everyone, rich and poor, the same money. Last time they taxed us, the rich paid more and the poor were only expected to provide a few pennies.'

He told her a story she had heard before, about how the plague had taken half the village and how those that remained thought their lives would be so much better afterwards. They would be free to demand greater wages and go and work for a lord who would pay them properly, and treat them with respect. But that never happened. Laws were quickly passed forbidding pay rises and farm labourers were not allowed to move from one manor to another in search of better work. The more Thomas spoke, the angrier he felt. Tilda began to feel he might be persuaded to join the rebels after all.

As they ate their oaty stew, Tilda asked her father about the things the rebel villeins had said. Thomas looked pensive. 'They're right, in a lot of ways. It's wrong that we are born serfs and that we're not allowed to sell our labour for a fair price. Really, we're slaves to the lord of the manor. I don't say that people are wrong to protest...' He looked pained. 'We live a bearable life here though, don't we, Tilda? I look after you all right. We're not starving are we? And we have a roof over our head, even if it is a leaky one.

'And Laybourne, he's an arrogant man, to be sure. What lord of the manor isn't? But he has not been pressing me to marry again. Many a lord would do that to his serfs – they all want us peasants to be fruitful and multiply. But he knew how much I loved my Mary. He'll be wanting to match you up soon enough though, Tilda. So don't be too fussy choosing a boy. Or you might find one chosen for you.'

Tilda had been told about this fairly recently. But she had dismissed it as a tease. Then it had slowly dawned on her that her father was being serious. She thought of the local boys with some revulsion and felt a great burst of anger. How could the lord possibly tell her to marry someone she had no wish to even speak to? The thought of it made her want to escape more than ever.

Now, she just stared at the floor, fearful of catching her father's eye and letting him see what she was really thinking. It was true what Thomas said, but if they were paid fairly for their labour, they would be able to afford to ask the thatcher to repair their roof, and have a constantly burning fire in their living area rather than a brief blaze to cook their food. That Laybourne – he had four fires in his manor house and smoke rose from the chimneys at every hour of the day.

There were so many things they could do if they had a little more money. She could even go to school, Tilda thought excitedly. She was desperate to learn how to read. She particularly wanted to read the Bible. She had long suspected there was knowledge there that was being kept from them. Ever since she was a little girl she had been puzzled about why some catastrophes were the work of the devil and some were because God was angry. God was angry when the plague came, but the devil was responsible for the failure of the harvest. Surely it was the farmer – the lord of the manor and his bad planning – rather than the devil? It was the devil too, who had ensured the war with France had gone on for so long and so fruitlessly. Tilda knew this was nonsense and she wanted to read the Holy Book for herself.

Those squiggly lines couldn't be that difficult to read. The local priest could read, after all, and he was no cleverer than the rest of them. And she'd seen Laybourne's three boys with books in their hands since they were children. Being able to read would be a truly wonderful thing, she thought.

'You're a funny one, Tilda,' said her father fondly. 'Lost in your thoughts... what are you thinking about?'

Tilda smiled. 'I'm thinking that we live in interesting times, Father. And maybe we have the chance of a better life ahead of us.'

CHAPTER FIVE

June 8, 1381

The week wound on, and in some ways it was as similar as any week in early June. There were no storms and the weather continued bright and fresh. Trees were budding and the fields were full of life. Hawks hunted, birds looked for worms for their young, and rabbits bobbed in and out of the grass. The renewal of the earth filled Tilda with hope, and even though they had the same meal every day for three days she was still happy. But she could sense that a great change was in the air.

What was different were the stories of further rebellion that continued to filter back to the village.

Across the Thames estuary, in Essex, tax collectors had been killed, they heard. Eustace Fogg was especially pleased to hear that his brother Peter was still free and prominent among the rebels, visiting neighbouring villages to gain support. In Essex, they heard, a large group of peasants had gathered, almost the size of an army. And it was not just the poorest of the land that had risen up. The clever people, the ones who were not lords but could read and had jobs that made use of their brains rather than their backs, many of them had also joined too.

When they took a break from harrowing the field, Tilda and Thomas were joined by Alan Carter, another neighbour and friend of Peter and Eustace Fogg.

'Every day something happens that shows the world is changing,' said Alan. 'A few days ago, a farmhand in Chilmington ran away from his manor, like we'd all like to do, in search of a better position and wage. They arrested him, put him in the local gaol, but a whole mob of his friends came and broke down the door of the gaol and set him free.' Alan could hardly contain his excitement.

'But aren't they worried they'll be punished?' said Thomas.

'This is happening all over the county,' said Alan. 'Look, I heard they broke into Maidstone Gaol, and set the prisoners free.'

Tilda was all ears. 'The more this happens the less they'll be able to punish us for standing up for what's right,' she said. 'They can't hang us all. There'll be no one left to till the fields and herd the cattle.'

Thomas was perplexed. 'But just going into gaols... that can't be right. For sure there are good men, Peter Fogg is a good man, I know for myself. But they have men in gaol for terrible things. For killing children, for rape, for highway robbery.'

'Father, the ones who have committed terrible crimes are usually hanged within a week, aren't they?' said Tilda. 'So perhaps most of the men they free are there because they shouldn't be?'

'If only life were that simple,' said Thomas. 'There are bound to be murderers and violators among them. The rebels will have that on their conscience if such men do something terrible.'

Seeing them talking together, another neighbour came to join them, anxious to learn the latest news. He has his own news too.

'The Kent rebels, they've even got their own leader. Wat Tyler he's called. He's going from village to village, stirring things up. He's calling on us all to march to London to talk to the king. Imagine that. A common man, set up as a prince among the common people. Much better than having to obey the miserable maggots who were born into their wealth and power, isn't that so?'

Such talk was plainly treasonous, thought Tilda, but it excited her more than she could imagine. It was undoubtedly true, unless you believed God had ordained the leaders personally and it was his will they reign over us. Tilda thought about that for a moment and decided it was too convenient. Bad kings and nobles had been killed and other kings had seized the throne. She had heard enough of those stories. This 'God-given authority' was obviously something you could just use to suit your argument.

The new arrival had something else to tell them. 'And John Ball has been freed from gaol too.' For

Tilda this was the most exciting news so far. John Ball, the preacher whose words had so inspired her. That was extraordinary.

'The world is changing every day,' she said to them all. 'We have to join this crowd going to London.'

Thomas was still doubtful. 'But what of Lord Laybourne?' he said. 'He and his officers will know we have abandoned our village. He will punish us.'

'Laybourne has gone,' said Alan. 'He took his family and servants down to Dover this morning. I saw them leaving with a big cart of furniture and their dogs and a few hens and pigs. There's been no smoke from the chimneys today. They say he's sailing up to Yorkshire, where he has further estates.'

That was extraordinary news too. Today was a day full of wonders. But with nothing else to do, and food to grow to fill their bellies, they all returned to their labours.

*

Late afternoon, just when the shadows were growing longer and Tilda and Thomas were thinking of finishing their harrowing and tilling for the day, they were disturbed yet again by the arrival of a large crowd.

'Exciting times, Father!' said Tilda. She had never seen so many comings and goings in Aylesford in her life.

At the head of this column of villeins was a hearty, thickset fellow who oozed confidence and intelligence. The new arrivals gathered in the field closest to the village huts and called for all around to come and listen to their message.

'Brothers,' said their leader. 'I can see you are all good, God-fearing men. Come and join us! We proclaim our loyalty to the king. We are not traitors and God's anointed leader of our realm will understand that. Who among you is happy with their lot? Who is happy to be a serf to the lord for the rest of their lives? Who is happy for the tax collectors to come on a whim to take a week's wages?'

No one called out to disagree although plenty were smiling and willing the man on to say more. Tilda looked around to see if she could see Walter and Elspeth Cooper. Maybe they too had fled, when they heard Laybourne had gone and they could no longer count on his protection. Tilda doubted anyone would kill them but they might beat them badly. The Coopers had been telling the lord and his constables of petty thefts and derelictions of duty for years. They certainly had plenty of enemies.

'It is not the king we rise against, but his courtiers,' continued the head of the crowd. 'He is surrounded by poor advisors who drip poison in his ear. You all know the names – Gaunt, Hales, Sudbury and the rest. Everyone knows they are greedy bloodsuckers. Enriching themselves while we live in rags with never enough food in our bellies...

'This very day we have been to Rochester and the castle opened their doors before us. The guards fled and we set the prisoners free.'

Here everyone cheered. Thomas looked wary. 'All the prisoners?' he said under his breath to Tilda.

'Follow us,' the man continued. 'Every village from here to Maidstone is marching to London to protest against our slavery and our overbearing, greedy rulers.

'Come, gather provisions and water to drink and we shall march on London. God will provide – and if he doesn't there are many manor houses on our way with bursting pantries. They will not dare to deny us food.'

The crowd cheered these rebellious words, growing bolder by the moment.

'Who is that man?' Thomas asked. 'He looks like a soldier.'

'We were talking about him earlier,' said Eustace. 'His name is Wat Tyler.'

Tilda hung on to her father's sleeve. She was grinning with excitement. Thomas looked stern. 'It's our lives we're risking here, Tilda. If we're lucky we'll be hanged. If we're unlucky we'll be hanged, drawn and quartered.'

But Tilda sensed this was not the time to be meek. 'Father, when will we ever have the chance to do this again?'

Someone else was calling out, 'We can be in London in three or four days. And the sooner we get there, the sooner we will be able to feast on the riches of the city.'

'What's the worst that can happen?' Tilda said. 'We'll be executed. It's worth the risk for a better life.'

'I'm not going, Tilda. And I shall not let you go either.'

The man they thought was Wat Tyler declared, 'You are either with us or against us! Come, swear an oath of loyalty to our cause.'

One of the rebels standing close to him said, 'Come, or we shall burn your own huts to the ground. Come, or you will be traitors to your fellow countrymen.'

Tilda and Thomas looked at each other, horrified. Was this the choice before them? They had to commit treason or be killed by their fellow rebels. They looked at Tyler to see what he would say. But at that moment another of the Rolfe's neighbours called out, 'The lord has gone. He's run away!'

Tyler's face lit up. 'Then we must go at once to his manor house and burn it to the ground. Is that where all your records are kept? Is that where the contracts for your rent and bonds of service are held? Come. You have not an instant to loose!'

With a great cheer everyone in the village swept at once towards the manor house. As they hurried, Tilda looked at her father. He in turn, looked perturbed. 'What can we do?' he said to her. 'If we don't come with them, will the rebels regard us as traitors and turn on us?'

Within minutes there were fifty or sixty people banging on the doors of the great stone building. As they approached, they had seen two people jump from an upper-floor window and run over the field next to the house. Tilda did not recognise them but assumed they must be a couple of servants left behind to ensure the house was not broken into. They might have been effective against a couple of burglars, but were no protection against a rowdy mob.

The door was too sturdy to yield, so someone smashed the glass window frame next to it. He wriggled into the house and opened the door from the inside.

Being inside the manor house felt like the wickedest thing Tilda had ever done in her life. All around were things that the Rolfes and their ilk could never dream of having in their homes. There were beautiful tapestries on the walls – so old the colours had faded, but still fascinating to see. There were sturdy pots and pans in the kitchen – silver and pewter, with brass ladles and serving spoons. Nothing like the meagre earthenware pots and wooden spoons that the Rolfes made use of. The great wooden chests and chairs and tables were of the finest quality. Even the candlestick holders were elaborate and beautiful to behold. Tilda wondered what they had taken with them, if these wonderful riches were what they had left behind. She had never felt so unsettled in her life. Any moment now she expected Laybourne or one of his arrogant sons to return and slay them all with a sword for trespassing.

Ahead lay a polished wooden staircase of carved, dark wood. Mesmerised by its magnificence for a moment she dashed up it, ever conscious of the fact that she was placing herself even further away from the door and a quick escape if anyone should come demanding to know what they were doing.

At the top of the stairs was a large landing with a beautiful ornate carpet and several rooms running off it. One of them had its door half open and Tilda was drawn inside. The room was obviously Lady Laybourne's. Beautiful red and green dresses with fur-trimmed collars lay spread out on a plump four-poster bed, with drawn-back velvet curtains on every side. On a table by the window was a looking glass and several colourful bottles. All this glass fascinated Tilda. They had glass in the windows. Imagine that. Looking out over the fields from a high spot and not being able to feel a chill draft.

It was strange being alone in this room. Downstairs was utter commotion and she could hear banging and shouting and smashing of glass and furniture. Someone had started on the kitchen crockery too, methodically smashing plates one at a time.

Tilda wanted to steal the looking glass. It was small enough to carry but no villein would have such a thing in their house and it would be too obvious that it had been stolen. In a strange still moment, Tilda held it up. She was fascinated to see her reflection – something she had only seen before looking down into a still pond or a large bowl of water when she had to hold her hair away from her face. Now here she was looking straight ahead at her face, the way others would see her. She liked what she could see. And she did have a magnificent head of curly black hair. She put the looking glass down, feeling a great twinge of regret that she was not able to take it.

The other bottles fascinated her too. She picked one up and removed the stopper... the smell was literally indescribable. Tilda had heard of the odour of sanctity – the heavenly smell that was supposed to fill a room when someone of saintly virtue died, an archbishop perhaps, or a really pious king. Maybe it was like this? She sniffed again at the bottle and tried to work out what was in this extraordinary scent. There was a strong smell of flowers but something more than that too. She thought of herbs and spices like cloves and cardamom, the sort of things they put in expensive pies. Perhaps it was something of that as well, but sweeter.

Tilda had never stolen anything in her life but she found herself putting the bottle in her pocket, her hand drawn almost like an invisible force. There was a drawer on the table too, and she opened it guiltily. The Laybournes had left in a terrible hurry it seemed. Lady Laybourne had even left some of her jewellery behind. There in the drawer were several sets of earrings – silver and gold inset with the most beautiful gemstones. I could never wear these, thought Tilda to herself – everyone would know they were stolen. She slammed the drawer shut and tried to put the sight of the beautiful stones out of her mind. Her father called up the stairs, 'Tilda, come quickly. They are going to set the house alight.'

Tilda felt a sense of outrage. She dashed to the landing and called downstairs. 'But this beautiful house will make a home for several of us. This is a cruel waste. And what of these tapestries and curtains and blankets. Surely they will make our lives better in the village.'

'You've taken leave of your senses, girl,' someone shouted up. 'When Laybourne returns with armed men, and goes from hut to hut with his overseers seeing what has been stolen... he'll see his curtains and his blankets and you'll hang for sure.'

'Or have your hands chopped off,' someone else yelled.

It was a fair point. All of them in the village, they had so little. Anything with even a hint of luxury would point them straight to the hangman's noose.

Now she could smell burning and smoke was beginning to drift up the stairs and catch in her throat. It was time to go.

On a sudden impulse Tilda rushed back into the bedroom and over to Lady Laybourne's jewellery drawer. She grabbed a handful of the most colourful earrings – the blue, the green, the red – and stuffed them into her pocket before running down the stairs.

The mob stood and watched the fire catch, spreading from the kitchen to the rest of the ground floor along the wooden floors and wood-panelled walls. Next to a ground-floor window was a great bonfire of parchment rolls and wooden boxes. These must be the records that showed they were Laybourne's serfs and how much they had paid him in rent for their humble little hovels. Seeing those burn made Tilda feel light-headed.

But now she had had enough. She took her father by the hand and they walked back to the village. She could see he was scanning the fields and hedgerows. 'No sign of the Coopers,' she said.

'I think I saw them running away when the mob arrived,' said Thomas. 'They might have been watching everything from afar.' Tilda wondered if they'd seen her staring out of Lady Laybourne's bedroom window. If they told the Laybournes that, they would know she had stolen the earrings. She felt a twisted anxiety. Was it fear or was it guilt? Maybe a mixture of the two. She decided not to tell her father about the jewellery. It would have to be her own little secret.

By the time they got back home, the burning manor house was blazing from top to bottom and a plume of black smoke reached high into the blue sky.

'I have a confession to make,' said Tilda as they stood and watched. She took out the bottle of perfume she had taken from the manor house.

Thomas took the stopper from the bottle, smelt it, then smiled sadly. 'How your mother would have loved such a heavenly scent,' he said. 'But you know we can't keep it, don't you?'

'I thought we could leave it at the Coopers – somewhere not too obvious?'

Thomas grinned. 'We could!'

Then his face took on a more serious air. 'I hate them, Tilda. But they could be hanged or lose a limb for that. I don't want that on my conscience, do you?'

'I'll keep it with me, then. It might come in useful.'

'You can't use it though, dearing. No villein would ever smell like that.'

That evening, over their usual stew, Tilda was bursting with impatience. 'We have to join the rebels, Father,' she said. 'Especially after this afternoon. It's going to be terrifying when Laybourne gets back.'

Much to her surprise he agreed. 'Very well, we shall go. I shall come with you to make sure you are safe.'

CHAPTER SIX

June 11, 1381

Guy de Clare peered east from the walls of Windsor Castle to the distant spires and smoking chimneys of London. He was enjoying this moment of solitude, alone in a high tower. The sun was hot on his face and a cooling fresh breeze blew in from the north. Guy winced at this hazy view of London – a hot day like this would only increase the miasma of that overcrowded, dangerous place. Guy had grown up in Gloucestershire and he had had an abiding dislike of the stink and bustle of cities ever since he had visited them as a child. He wished he was back home there now, with his brothers and sisters in the security of the family manor house. Today would be a perfect day to go fowling, hunting with his dogs and his bow and arrow. He thought longingly of his childhood friends and how much he missed those simple, uncomplicated attachments.

Today he had to do again what he had had to do for the last terrifying month. In a moment, he needed to return to the vast vaulted throne room and sit in the court where he was a scribe for King Richard. Here he would be watching the flattering and scheming and cutting remarks. The etiquette of the court, the possibility of humiliation and constant pressure not to do the wrong thing, weighed heavily upon him.

When he had arrived those long four weeks ago, he had hoped he would like Richard. The boy's father, the Black Prince, was the stuff of legend. This was the man who had personally captured the King of France in battle, the man who was a byword for chivalric manliness. Guy shuddered at his own naivety, imagining that perhaps his son, the current king, would be cut from the same cloth. Well, maybe the first-born Edward was. But that boy had died aged five, and now second-born Richard had been king for four years, his coronation at a mere ten years old. And whatever Richard was like, he was nothing like his father. This fourteen-year-old king was lanky, blond and boyish, almost like a girl. And his character was entirely not to Guy's liking. Capricious, imperious, aloof. Guy tried to sympathise, imagining what it must be like to have that power and responsibility at such a young age. It was not difficult for him to do – he was fourteen too, and similarly tall and fair. He wondered sometimes if this was why Richard had chosen him. He also wondered if Richard liked having him close by in case an assassin mistook Guy for himself. That had given him a few sleepless nights.

But despite it all, he lived in fear of being sent home, rejected by the court. Guy loved his father, a knight in the service of the Earl of Northumbria, and when the earl asked, at Richard's request, if he could have a bright boy to work in the court as a scribe, Guy was a perfect match. Even at fourteen he spoke four languages: English and French, Latin and Spanish. And he was a sensible, grown-up sort of young man. That's how he liked to appear to the world, anyway. No one must know how frightened he was of his courtly duties.

Deep in thought, he did not notice the small cloud of dust on the road leading to the castle until the rider was perhaps half a mile away. He was driving his horse on with his riding whip, and clearly in a terrible hurry. Now Guy could hear the rhythm of the horse's hooves. Below, a grand gate was opened and the rider slowed to enter. Guy hurried to the court, certain that urgent news was about to be delivered to the king. And it was not difficult to guess what it might be. News of various rebellions out in the shires had been filtering through over the last two weeks. The council that advised the young king seemed unconcerned, and were sure the unruly activity would settle down – especially as the villeins knew how fierce the penalties for rebellion would be. But this advice was looking increasingly flawed.

*

The stone-vaulted throne room was flooded with light from great windows on either side. This room was like the side chapel of a grand church, and it was full of the most powerful men in England. On a raised platform at the far end of the room sat Richard in his finery, surrounded by three of the counsel – whose duty it was to advise him until he was old enough to rule alone. Also there was his mother, Joan of Kent. She was fifty now, but still beautiful. There was a distinct resemblance and it was obvious to all that Richard took after her rather than the Black Prince.

The rest of the long room was full of lesser courtiers, further advisors, Joan's ladies-in-waiting, and servants to tend to their needs. Although it was a warm day, the fires at either side of the room were lit, to keep off the cold from the stone floors and walls. Carpets and rugs covered some of the floor and rich tapestries hung from the small wall space between the windows.

A herald blew a trumpet and a tall military man entered. He bowed solemnly and walked with urgency towards the throne.

'What news have you?' enquired the king in his reedy, recently broken voice. Guy noticed there were red spots on his otherwise creamy complexion.

'Your Majesty, my lord, Sir William Walworth, Lord Mayor of London, sends news of further revolts in the shires, most especially in Kent and Essex.'

Richard shrugged. 'The lord mayor has sent many messages such as this. Why have these revolts not been suppressed?'

'I cannot answer that, Your Majesty,' said the messenger. 'But these revolts have now taken on a more alarming form. Sir Robert Belknap, arriving to preside over the Dartford Assizes, has been seized by rebels. Justices of the peace, constables, revenue collectors and other representatives of His Majesty's authority have been foully murdered. Rochester Castle has been seized...'

Richard could not contain himself and broke the deadly hush that had descended on the court.

'Rochester?' he exclaimed. 'But it's impregnable!'

'Yes, Your Majesty,' said the messenger. 'I understand the guards fled when the mob approached.'

Richard's mouth tightened to a grimace. He waved his hand to indicate that the man should continue.

'Rochester has been seized and the castle keeper Sir John Newton taken hostage. Maidstone Gaol has been ransacked and the heretic preacher John Ball has been freed.'

Guy de Clare glanced over at Archbishop Sudbury. The news plainly unsettled him. Ball had declared himself an enemy to the established church and had been stirring up hatred and outrage against its leaders. When his name was first mentioned, the court had dismissed him as an irritating crank. That had been a serious error. Guy saw Sudbury whispering in a courtier's ear. It was not hard to guess what he was saying. He would wager his favourite hunting dog that it involved hanging, drawing and quartering.

The messenger continued. 'Canterbury too has been infected by the rebellion. Throughout the two counties of Essex and Kent, manor houses are being ransacked and prisons attacked. Many felons have been released into the country. Disorder reigns. Most serious of all is the news that two armies of peasants are marching on London. My lord, the lord mayor requests your advice most urgently.'

Richard took in this news without giving any further indication of his true thoughts. He called out, 'Give this man food and water and a fresh horse.' Then he spoke directly to the messenger.

'Return to Sir William and tell him we will advise him presently.'

The horseman left the court and Richard announced, 'We must discuss this matter in more intimate surroundings.'

The king and his advisors, and Guy de Clare, who was charged with recording these matters, shuffled into an anteroom and sat around a great oak table. Guy waited for the meeting to begin, quill poised over parchment, ink at the ready. This time he had prepared well in advance and remembered with almost quivering shame the day last week when he had run out of ink.

For several weeks now these tales of rebellion had been filtering through from the shires. The cause was plain enough. The common people were objecting to the new poll tax being imposed upon them – a shilling – twelve pennies – from every person over the age of fifteen. Richard's advisors had been recommending a firm enforcement of royal authority. Examples must be made, ringleaders executed. Guy could not help but notice the court's contempt for the stinking, shoeless rustics. He felt more ambivalent about that. As a boy he had played with the children of peasants at his own family manor outside Northleach. Jack and Sam had been his best friends, hunting and fishing and exploring in the beautiful, undulating Gloucestershire countryside. He knew how different his life was from theirs, and how little they had in this world.

Since he had arrived at the court, Guy had struggled to remember it was not his place to say anything – even as he recorded on parchment, things he knew would lead to trouble and upheaval. The new poll tax, especially, was one where he had to bite his lip. The decision to levy it had happened before he had arrived at court, but the consequences of it had occupied many a council meeting since.

Guy understood how much an extra shilling per head would be resented. That was a week's wages for most of these people. And he knew they lived hand to mouth – uncertain whether there would be bread on the table from one day to the next. And to ask it equally from all the citizens of the land – regardless of their wealth and status – that was plainly unjust. Surely the council could see that? No one had said what he was screaming to say. That it was obvious why this had caused so much ill-feeling. But then he looked at all the council sitting around the table. Every last one of them wore the finest clothes. Hales wore a tunic lined with pearls, which must have cost more than a mere villein would earn in his entire life. A shilling meant nothing to these people. How could they understand what it meant to the men who ploughed the fields or threshed the corn?

And Guy knew first-hand what happened when you pushed the common people too far. When he was eight his uncle had been killed by disgruntled peasants over in Turkdean village when he had tried to intervene in a dispute over rents and tithes to be paid to the local abbey. Retribution was swift and fierce. Heads and hands were cut off. Families ruined. Guy's father had worried that his son might be killed in revenge, and for a whole year he had been forbidden to play outside the manor grounds. Guy had seen Jack and Sam at market days in Northleach after that and they had refused even to meet his eye. When he had tried to speak to them it was clear they both hated and feared him and his family.

But now, in this deepening crisis, Guy also wondered if it would be more prudent for the king to address the cause of these rebellions and discover what could be done to bring the upheaval to an end. In Gloucestershire, Guy had felt sympathy for the peasants, protest – knowing how poor they were. Wrong had clearly been done and he was sorry his uncle had had to die for a reason as unjust as that. He dared not say this to Richard of course, although he would do if the young king asked him his opinion. It hadn't happened yet, but sometimes, during these meetings, he caught Richard looking at him, and wondered if he was going to ask him what he thought.

When all the advisors had arrived, the meeting began. Richard declared, 'This is all most untimely. With our most valued advisor John of Gaunt away with his army in Scotland, we are facing this uprising with considerably fewer resources at our disposal.' He paused. 'But here is what we shall do. We shall head at once to London. We shall seek protection in the Tower. Any rebel army approaching the city shall be locked out. Then we will discover more of what is happening and how best to deal with it. Our inclination is to meet with the leaders of this revolt and determine what it is they want.'

'My lord,' cautioned the Duke of Norfolk. 'Would it not be safer for you to remain here at Windsor, and allow your emissaries to report on the situation?'

Richard was adamant. 'We may be a boy in years but we have the heart of a king, and a king should lead his people in times of danger. Make preparations to leave at once. What time are the tides today? We shall travel by water.'

The meeting ended. Guy was left with a grudging admiration for the young king. Here he was showing leadership and courage. He was heading straight into danger, rather than hiding from it. If the tides were running in their favour, they should be in London by evening. But then a sliver of fear settled in his gut. Wherever Richard went, he went too. Guy de Clare had never really been in any real danger at any point in his life. He sensed that this was about to change.

*

The royal river party arrived at the Palace of Westminster after a tense and rather tedious journey, battling against the tide. Guy had been here before but he was still impressed by the palace's sturdy crenellated walls and grand halls. He was pleased to be off the crowded boat. It was the latest in water-borne luxury, to be sure, bedecked with lustrous tapestries to ward off the stiff river breezes. But three hours bobbing about with those breezes was quite enough for him. They stayed at the palace a bare hour, enough to eat and drink and hear the latest news. It was bad and getting worse. 'Your Majesty, we hear large groups of rustics continue to approach from both Kent and Essex,' said Lord Treasurer Hales.

Lord Chancellor Sudbury could not hide his anxiety and fretted constantly with the sides of his hat. 'We are ill-equipped to deal with them,' he said gravely. 'With armies away in Portugal and Scotland we have fewer than a thousand men here in the capital.'

Richard appeared peevish. Perhaps, thought Guy, he had found the river journey tiresome too. He seemed especially irritable with his chief advisors, looking at them with hood-eyed contempt when they spoke. He gave the clear impression that it was their fault he was in the mess he was in, although he wasn't going to say so out loud. Guy wondered if this was because he didn't want anyone to remind him that he himself had approved both the dispatching of troops to these faraway places and the imposing of the taxes that had caused so much unrest.

Sudbury had a clear idea of what they needed to do. 'We must leave here at once and go to the Tower – it is the safest place for us all.'

Richard spoke. 'My Lord Chancellor – these are my very thoughts,' he said. 'In the Tower we will be safe from the fury of the mob. But we do not have enough soldiers to take the fight to them. Instead, we must discover what they want. That is why we should go to talk to them and determine what they hope to achieve.'

Guy wanted to speak but knew he was not allowed to. They might kill you, he thought. And as I am going to be with you, they'll kill me too. But he chastised himself for such unmanly thoughts.

'Your Majesty is most gallant,' said Lord Treasurer Hales. 'But might I suggest our best strategy for now is to wait until we are more fully informed.'

Richard nodded, the contempt he had been showing momentarily on hold. Guy thought he caught a glimpse of relief flash across the king's face. Richard had said what he thought he ought to say. He was happy to agree with a more cautious approach. 'Yes. We shall do this. And we shall wait in the Tower. It is much nearer to the mobs.' He waved a hand in a circular motion, something he often did when he was thinking, 'Meanwhile, instruct the guardians of London Bridge to raise their drawbridge when the mob approaches.'

'My lord, that will not prevent the entry of the Essex mob,' said Sudbury.

Richard looked irritated. 'Indeed not, Lord Chancellor,' he snapped. 'But it will leave us with fewer rebels to deal with. And perhaps some of the Kent mob will drown in the Thames if they attempt to swim across the river.' He stopped to snigger at this suggestion. 'And send out messengers to address the crowd. Tell them to go home.'

Richard's advisors tried to hide their surprise at this final suggestion. They bowed and said this would be done forthwith. Ten minutes later Richard and his entourage were back on the Thames.

Guy had always enjoyed the river trip into the heart of the city, watching with fascination as scattered houses on the riverside became denser and the city began in earnest. There was always something going on right on the bank – from tanners to iron refineries, breweries to blacksmiths. But today he felt too distracted and a chill passed through him as the looming walls of the Tower of London came into sight. But he was also comforted to be there. With its sturdy outer walls and great white inner tower it seemed like the safest place in London.

CHAPTER SEVEN

June 12, 1381

The journey to the edge of London had been hard. Tilda had never walked so far away from home. Her feet ached and she was desperate to wash her clothes and clean herself up. But she was far from unhappy. She had never experienced such a feeling of power in her life. Being part of this large group of people, all armed with a weapon of some sort, was immensely exciting. She felt herself growing taller every day.

The farm workers had taken their scythes and pitchforks, and anyone who was a former soldier or who had such a weapon at home carried bow and arrows, swords and pikes. On the way they had ransacked country manor houses and pillaged the larger homes in small towns to provide them with provisions for their journey. Any lords and ladies, tax collectors and government officers foolish enough to find themselves on their path had been attacked and beaten. Some Tilda heard, had been murdered. But such incidents had been rare. Most of the king's servants fled before the approaching mob. But there was no looting. The rebels had maintained their promise of good behaviour – they made it plain to all that they were seeking justice, not booty. They had only taken bread and meat from the houses they had attacked, although some had also been burned to the ground. And local records offices, full of manuscripts relating to tax payments, rents and other services demanded of the local population, had been a special target.

Best of all, in every place they had swept through, people had joined them. And not just the farming men and women – the villeins like them. Judging by the conversations Tilda overheard around her, many of these people were learned – people with an education. People who could read. She realised then, with some relief, that this rebellion had every chance of succeeding. The king and his advisors had caused the entire country to rise up against them – not just the lowly peasants. Perhaps her father was thinking as much too. Thomas smiled at her and put a protective arm round her shoulder. 'I'm glad you persuaded me to come, my dearing,' he said. 'This is truly the greatest event of our life.'

Now, on this fine summer morning, they climbed a long hill and found themselves on Blackheath – a flat plain about the size of a large farm. On the way up the hill Thomas told Tilda that this was where the London dead of the plague had been buried. Tilda expected it to be a sinister place, but there in the sunshine it seemed a perfectly pleasant spot to spend an hour resting. Here were thousands of people – more than she had ever seen in her life. It was here that she realised how massive this protest had become. But the crowd was strangely quiet, tired from their journey and perhaps realising that their hour was coming. The quiet hung over them, like a great weight of air.

Tilda sensed something just out of sight, almost like an animal senses danger. She could smell it on the wind, and maybe even hear, just on the threshold of sound, the hum of the great city. She knew her father had been to London before. He had been allowed to go there for his brother's wedding. Tilda could tell that he was excited to be going back. Now he took her arm and they ran towards the northern side of the heath, detaching themselves from the great crowd.

Here they found themselves on the brim of a steep hill. Tilda had never seen anything like it. Below was the River Thames, narrow enough now for a strong swimmer to cross from one bank to the other. On the far side were small settlements – little groups of houses here and there, but nothing you could call a village. On their side of the river was a hunting lodge – grand enough to be a royal dwelling. But further in the distance was a great grey mass. There were spires, bridges, castle towers, and thousands of tiny houses, all swirling in the heat haze and smoke from innumerable chimneys. One great spire especially stood out, pointing boldly at the sky. She couldn't believe what she was seeing. 'How do so many people live there all together?' she marvelled. Then she asked,

'And why do they need fires on a day like today?' Thomas shrugged. 'Blacksmiths, bakeries, lime-burning... all sorts going on down there.'

'What happens now, Father?' asked Tilda. Seeing the vast city had made her anxious. 'We've got to go there, haven't we?'

Thomas took her arm. 'Come on, back to the crowd. We don't want to miss anything.' They arrived on the fringe to see the radical preacher John Ball in full flow. He was a distant figure, standing on a wooden cart, surrounded by thousands of people. And even though he was shouting at the top of his voice, and the crowd were maintaining a respectful silence, it was difficult to hear him. Even when people in such a large crowd are silent, they still make a sound, in their shuffling and scratching.

But the words they could hear were reassuring. Ball told the rebels they were not traitors but 'with King Richard and the True Commons of England'. They were not there to overthrow the government. They were loyal Englishmen. A message had been sent to Richard, Ball told them, reassuring the king that the rebellion was not against him, but the traitors that surrounded him at court. When Ball finished, the crowd cheered him like a hero. Tilda was struck by the sense and reasonableness in his words. This world they lived in, with kings and dukes and lords and ladies, it wasn't there in the Garden of Eden. The way they lived now was plainly against God's will.

While they waited on the heath for others to speak to them, word went around the crowd that Richard had sent messengers telling the arrivals to go home. This seemed to increase the indignation of the people and their determination to be heard. Tilda heard one of the king's heralds had been driven off with a hail of stones. Another, she heard, had been set upon and beaten. But it was difficult to know what was true and what was hearsay.

Then Wat Tyler stepped up on to the cart. 'It's him,' cried Tilda. 'We saw him in Aylesford!'

Thomas hushed her and they both strained to hear his words.

At first he said much the same thing as John Ball. 'Remember, we come not as thieves and robbers. We come seeking justice.'

Tyler again called for the end to serfdom and the right to move at will around the country in search for well-paid work. But more worryingly he also had a list of the king's most important advisors and demanded that they be handed over to the protestors for punishment. Thomas shook his head and Tilda could clearly see her father was uneasy. But he did not call out to disagree. They could both sense the mood of the crowd and it was vengeful.

Thomas quietly confided in his daughter. He could not hide his indignation. 'This is not going to happen,' he said. 'The king will never hand over the chancellor, the treasurer, the keeper of the privy seal, and all those judges Tyler mentioned. He just won't do it. I'm sure half of them are related to him in some way. And if he did, the lords and ladies of the court would rise up against him.' He lowered his voice and whispered, 'I feel this will be our undoing, Tilda. We are being led by a fool.'

Tilda was not so sure. 'But these are the men who have advised the king to tax us all so unfairly. Isn't that what this uprising's all about – getting rid of people like that?' she said.

When Tyler stepped down, the great crowd cheered. Now, everyone was ready to push on to London. 'This is it, Tilda,' said Thomas. 'Whatever the king has got in store for us, we'll find out later today or tomorrow.'

'What do you mean?' asked Tilda. Her father had made her feel anxious again.

'So far, all the way from Aylesford, we have not once been in fear of our lives,' said Thomas. 'We have rebelled – merrily committed treason – and no one has come to punish us. Somewhere along the way we will be meeting soldiers loyal to their king. Surely they will try to catch us before we reach the city. We are out in the open here. Easy prey to a trained army. I'm surprised they have not been waiting for us here...'

'Maybe Richard is reassured by what the leaders have said,' said Tilda hopefully.

'Maybe,' says Thomas, eying the horizon. 'We shall have to see.'

Their discussion was interrupted by men in the crowd pealing small hand bells and calling for silence. Tyler was back on top of the wooden cart. 'We have received word that King Richard himself will meet us at Greenwich. We must all head down to the river.'

Everyone turned across the heath, and poured down the hill. More rumours swept through the crowd. The Earl of Buckingham had joined the rebels with his own army. The king's own mother, Joan of Kent, had given her blessing to the rebellion. Tilda wanted to be comforted by these wonderful things she was hearing. But she realised she could say anything to her companions here and it would spread through the crowd like wildfire. She had to suppress a mischievous urge to tell them that John of Gaunt had returned with his army and sworn allegiance to the rebel cause.

Within half an hour, thousands of peasants and townfolk were waiting expectantly by the river, eyeing the Thames for the first sign of a royal barge. Tilda and Thomas were right there on the river's edge, so close Tilda wanted to jump in and cool herself down. But the river flowed fast and she was no swimmer. Still, she was excited. She had never seen a king or queen before. This moment was so extraordinary she entirely forgot the fear that had gripped her earlier.

CHAPTER EIGHT

Guy De Clare had been awaiting this moment with great trepidation. Yesterday's journey from Windsor to Westminster and then the Tower of London had passed without incident. But when they got to the Tower the mood was sombre and Richard and his entourage had been told the rebels were already arriving at Blackheath. But Richard stayed true to his decision. 'We shall head there tomorrow morning and see for ourselves.'

Just as they were preparing to leave, a messenger came running up to the riverside. 'My lords,' he called out to the royal barge, which had already slipped its moorings. 'The rebels say they are with King Richard and the Commons of England.'

Richard looked quizzical. 'Are they indeed? We shall go and see for ourselves what these knaves are demanding.'

Even as they sailed downriver, his chief advisors Sudbury and Hales were counselling the king to turn back and send a heavily armed cohort of soldiers instead. The Lord High Treasurer, Robert Hales, declared, 'I will go to talk to these vermin and bring back the head of their leader.'

Richard looked on him with a slight degree of scorn. 'Lord High Treasurer,' he said. 'Your loyalty and courage cannot be faulted, but I should be most displeased if it were your head they took instead. Caution and cunning are what is required in these circumstances.'

Richard's advisors all murmured their assent. Guy de Clare looked on this haughty boy with fresh admiring eyes, fascinated to hear what he might say next. He had this total belief in himself. Guy had never seen it in anyone else. This complete sense that he was here to do God's will, and that God's will was that he, Richard, should sit upon the throne and rule over his subjects. Guy supposed that his coronation in Westminster Abbey and its extraordinary display of colour and ceremony, with hundreds of trumpets and the sound of thousands of Londoners in the cheering crowds that lined the processional route, would have made anyone think that. There was an undeniable power in such certainty. He hoped Richard never lost that – it would be the end of him.

But as the barge turned along Limehouse Reach and the great bend down to Deptford and Greenwich, a frisson of fear ran through the king's men. There in the distance they could see thousands of people lining the riverbank at Greenwich. As they grew nearer, the jeering and shouting became more intense. And this group of upstarts were all waving weapons. Some had swords and spears but many others carried the sort of implements a villein would use to tend the land. Not that it mattered. Guy had heard it was a scythe that had killed his uncle. An implement like that could kill a man just as surely as it could cut grass. He shuddered as he remembered the woodcut engraving he had seen; a scythe was the very implement the grim reaper employed to harvest souls.

The royal barge came to a halt within hailing distance of the riverbank, and drifted uncertainly in the current. Richard stared across the water at the people who had come to protest against his government.

'My lord, we must not get too close,' said Chancellor Sudbury. 'There is a great risk of injury if the villeins on the riverbank employ bows and arrows. They may even have crossbows.'

Richard nodded but said nothing. He went to the cabin at the stern of the barge and emerged shortly afterwards in full regal splendour. His crown glistened in the summer sun and his ermine robes looked magnificent. He stood boldly at the front of the barge and the oarsmen manoeuvred it around so the bow of the boat was facing head on to the south bank of the river.

He raised an arm and the crowd fell silent. Richard called out to them in his reedy fourteen-year-old voice. 'I am your king. What brings you here to my city?'

An unintelligible cacophony erupted from the thousands that lined the riverbank. Guy could see someone in the crowd trying to quieten everyone. He assumed it was so their leader could speak in one voice for them all, but it was impossible.

Everyone was shouting and no one could hear a thing.

The lords Sudbury and Hales went to stand in front of Richard in a magnanimous gesture of protection. Guy, who was standing nearby, felt obliged to stand with them and covered his eyes against the sun to scan the crowd for crossbow men. He wondered if he could spot a speeding crossbow bolt if it came towards him. He heard the chief advisors tell their king this situation was too dangerous. 'Look how angry they are,' said Hales. 'Even if the great majority mean you no harm, it only takes one villein with a crossbow to slay the King of England.'

Richard put a hand to his ear in a strangely theatrical gesture. 'This does not sound like anger, my lords. But it is certainly anarchy. They all speak at once. I cannot converse with a many-headed monster.'

Sudbury said, 'We must retire at once, Your Majesty. This situation cannot be to our advantage. Only the rebels'. If you go ashore to talk with them, nothing good will come of it. They will kill you or hold you to ransom.'

Richard was unsure. 'But my lord Sudbury,' he said. 'We cannot send men against them. We have too few to fight such a mob. There are only six hundred men at the Tower. That is our entire strength. The advantage is entirely with the mob. We must do what we can by reason.'

The crowd grew distinctly more hostile. The jeers overcame the more plaintive pleas for reason.

Richard looked over to the mob. One or two had begun to hurl their spears in anger at the barge, although they were landing harmlessly a safe distance away. 'Your Majesty, it is only a matter of moments before the bowmen begin to employ their weapons,' said the Lord Chancellor. 'We must turn around at once.'

Richard sensed caution was required and made a small gesture to the helmsman. The barge pulled away and as it gathered speed with the incoming tide up the river, a few arrows splashed into the water behind it.

*

They had not long arrived back at the Tower when messengers appeared. Guy heard a breathless herald, clearly distressed and exhausted from his journey, telling Richard and his advisors that the rebels had refused to disperse. Guy looked at Richard, expecting him to say something sarcastic – clearly this man had no idea that the king had just returned from his own encounter with the mob. But Richard stayed silent and nodded his understanding. Guy noticed the herald was covered in bruises, and blood had soaked some of his uniform. Clearly Richard had some compassion in his regal soul.

There was further alarming news too. The rebels were demanding that the king's most important advisors should be handed over to them. And they had a list of names.

Guy could see the effect this had on the king's entourage. Treasurer Hales and Chancellor Sudbury seemed especially alarmed. Guy wondered if they had ever thought through the consequences of their ideas. Perhaps they had thought the peasantry too ignorant to attach this poll tax to their particular names. If so, they had miscalculated mightily.

Then another thought occurred to him. These same men of the council had made other terrible mistakes too – it was they who had approved the war with France, a war that had cost the country a quarter of a million pounds with no victories and no territory gained. Money like that could have rebuilt half the kingdom. People didn't mind being taxed for wars that they won – everyone from the lowest milkmaid and butcher's boy, to the dukes and earls, liked a military victory. But stalemate and defeat bought pleasure to no one.

When Guy was home in Gloucester, and still played and feasted with his childhood friends, there were even rumours that money supposedly gathered for the king's campaigns in France had gone instead to the pockets of the chief councillors. It did no one any good to stir that much hate against them. But looking at these grand advisors, as they clustered around the king, Guy could sense their own invulnerability slipping away. They, like Richard, had allowed themselves to think that God had ordained their power and position and they were untouchable. He now seriously doubted this was so.

CHAPTER NINE

Tilda watched the barge disappear down the river with a mixture of awe and disappointment. She had actually seen the King of England with her own eyes. The king! The man God himself had ordained to rule the country. She felt privileged. If she had children, she realised, she would tell them, and her grandchildren, about the day she saw the King of England. 'What was he like?' they might ask with wide-eyed wonder. And she would say, 'I only saw him from a distance, but even then, he seemed incredibly clean. He had blond hair and a smooth face beneath a golden crown which glinted in the sun.'

But there was something all too human about this boy-king. She had expected him to have a voice like thunder rather than the reedy peal of a boy on the edge of manhood. Or that there would be some sort of heavenly glow around him. But he was just a boy – no more and no less than the spotty youths who teased her about her skill with a slingshot. For one traitorous moment she wondered if she could have hit the king with a stone from where she stood on the riverbank. That would indeed be an extraordinary story to tell – the day I killed the King of England.

But the whole meeting had been a disappointment. Tilda had enjoyed being part of this mighty gang of angry people – knitted together by a righteous cause. But when the king had hailed them, they had all bellowed their needs at once, like the unruly mob they were. If they had the power to resist the soldiers that were sure to be sent against them, then they would have to behave like a proper army. To obey the commands of their officers. Tilda pictured Wat Tyler, impotently yelling at the crowd to be silent so he alone could converse with the king. Tyler had bellowed himself hoarse. It was almost comical. This was a chance they had missed. Who knew when they would have another one.

By now it was late afternoon and the crowd were weary. They began to settle on the hill away from the river, some eating the last of the provisions they had pillaged on their way. Others combing the crowd were begging plaintively for scraps of food. Tomorrow, the word went round, they would march on London.

Tilda and Thomas both felt exhausted. 'Let us rest a while, daughter,' he said and they lay down in the lush grass of the hill that rose above the riverbank. Tilda watched small clouds drift lazily across the great blue sky and her own thoughts began to drift too.

She thought especially about what the future held in store. All her life she had been told that her fate was to marry a silly, swaggering Aylesford boy. Sometimes girls her age got married. She thought that was awful. Marriage, she knew, meant coupling. Her friend Cecily had told her about that. And coupling meant babies, unless you were lucky and never had any children. But then that wasn't really lucky either. Married couples who had no children were sometimes told to remarry by the lord of the manor. He wanted bodies to work on his land and boys and girls to sell along with his fields and animals if he ever decided to move away from the area.

Tilda had seen that with a kind couple who had looked after her when her mother had died. Joseph and Rose, they were called. The two of them were told to marry other people, as ten years of wedlock had produced no children. They pleaded with Lord Laybourne and told him they loved each other. But he was unmoved. Tilda realised how much she hated him when she heard that Rose was often beaten black and blue by her new husband Jeffery – a brute from Ditton, a nearby village Laybourne also owned. Joseph had fought with him because of it and Jeffery had beaten him almost half to death. The next day Joseph had disappeared and no one knew, even to this day, whether he had killed himself from shame or run away to another part of the country. Rose too had fared badly from this arrangement. Her belly had indeed swollen up with child but she and the newborn had both died when she gave birth. Tilda well remembered that night.

Poor Rose had gone to her mother's to have the child and her screams could be heard throughout the village.

So motherhood, or at least the process of it, terrified her. She loved little babies as much as the next village girl. They all gathered to coo at any new arrival in the village, but Tilda knew more than anyone her age how dangerous it was to have a child. Her dead mother still haunted her dreams.

Tilda thought about the other girls and women in the village. Some of them had had six or seven children by the time they were twenty-five. Not all of those children had lived though. As well as the awful danger of having a child there was the heartache of raising a little baby only to have it die.

Thomas stirred from his rest and interrupted her train of thought. 'Tilda, my dearing, we'll not stay here tonight. My brother John lives a mere two hours away. Will your feet carry you?'

Tilda considered it. True she was sore from the days walking behind her, but the prospect of spending a night indoors, with relatives who might offer a hot meal, was a very good reason to make a last effort. And she was intrigued to meet this branch of the family. Her father often spoke of his brother, who had moved to London to become a housebuilder.

They walked along the meadows close to the riverbank, the stench and size of London becoming more apparent in the late afternoon light. 'How can this many people live in one small spot?' marvelled Tilda. She thought longingly of the fresh air and wide-open fields of Aylesford.

Tilda had been in towns before, and had even visited Canterbury once, when she was twelve. But she felt overwhelmed whenever she approached such a great collection of houses and people. Aylesford was so small and insignificant in comparison. In a big town or city it was easy to feel like a little ant about to be crushed under the heels of a giant.

As their tired feet carried them the last few miles towards London, however, she sensed that this was going to be like nowhere else she had ever been. For a start, most towns, and Canterbury of course, had great towering church spires or towers. The towers at Canterbury Cathedral were so vast you could see them a day's walk away. Here in

London there were so many spires and towers it was impossible to count them. And the whole city seemed to be covered in a haze of smoke. There was a great cathedral towering over everything else. Thomas told her it was called St Paul's. It had a huge, pointed spire that almost touched the clouds. Even from outside the city it looked so big and solid that Tilda could only wonder how it was not swallowed by the earth it rested on. She wondered what it would be like to climb to the top of it and see the world as a bird sees it.

And the smell was like nothing she had ever experienced in her life. Even on Blackheath they had sensed it in an occasional whiff on the wind, but the closer they got the more intense it became. They were near enough now to notice the ground around them littered with debris – everything from piles of rotten wood and discarded furniture to animal bones. Dogs and pigs rooted around, some eagerly digging their jaws into rotting meat, indifferent to the clouds of flies that had settled there. Great fat rats scurried in and out of the rubble, unafraid of the other creatures around them. There were piles of human waste here too. And worse. Among the debris of the city were human remains. Bodies strung up on gallows, left to rot as a warning to anyone entering the city with criminal intent. Tilda shuddered at their grinning skulls, all that was left of faces picked clean by crows. Some of these dangling bodies were so withered by the elements, you could see the blackened sinews and yellowing bones beneath their decaying clothes. Tilda suppressed an urge to retch and longed for the fresh air and fields of Kent.

'Tilda, my dearing,' said Thomas, taking her hand. 'You must keep your eyes on the ground ahead of you.' She looked down, as stray turds and glistening white animal entrails marked the route ahead. It was difficult finding a path between them and the muddy puddles that dotted the ground.

Now the buildings on the outskirts of the city were clustered closer together, and all at once Thomas and Tilda were surrounded by urchin children begging for food and money, or demanding to know if they needed a room for the night. Tilda searched the faces of these children, none of whom seemed to be older than seven or eight, and sensed something hard and desperate in their eyes. She had never seen children this filthy and ragged – even among the poorest villeins of her village. Some of these urchins had eyes sunk deep in their sockets and skin stretched tight across their bony faces. They were obviously starving and if she had had any food left from their journey she would have given it to them.

Not all of London was sewer smells though. There was much here that excited her. There was fresh baked bread and cinnamon cakes and the warm fug of coal fires. There were shops too – still open in this early evening hour, selling all sorts, from pins to hot pies. Strangest of all for Tilda was the sensation of hearing people in the street who spoke another language. That was almost as strange as seeing people of different colour – not many to be sure, but among the bustling throng Tilda saw black faces for the first time in her life.

'We've timed our arrival well,' said Thomas. 'Soon it will be curfew, and we will need to be indoors by then.'

Tilda had heard of this – all big towns and cities had a curfew, when all sensible people would retire to their resting places and anyone caught outside who was not known to the nightwatchmen as a person of good character would be arrested and held overnight in gaol.

For now, shops were still open and street stalls still had their wares on display. Thomas haggled with a baker, eventually paying half of the price originally demanded for a small loaf. But it was still double what you would pay in Aylesford. He shrugged as they walked away. 'We can't turn up at John's house empty-handed,' he said. Tilda felt a twinge of disappointment – she was so hungry she wanted to eat the bread immediately.

Thomas pulled Tilda back as a cart lumbered down the road towards the narrowing street that seemed to be the main thoroughfare into the city. Small herds of sheep and even a handful of cattle, together with drivers anxious not to lose them, battled for space among the now cluttered streets. Tilda gripped her father's hand tightly. 'It would be a horrible nightmare getting lost in this,' she told him.

But there was something amazing about the scene before her eyes. In Aylesford, if you needed something, you had to make it yourself, or walk for a day to the nearest town to buy it. Here, if you had the right money, you could buy everything from a pair of scissors or needle and thread to a pretty red blanket or a bright yellow dress, all within a minute's walk along a crowded street.

And there was something else Tilda noticed at once. People were staring at them, sometimes with contempt – or was it pity? – in their eyes.

'They know we don't belong here, don't they?' she said. Their dowdy russet peasant clothes marked them out in a parade of brilliant colours and styles. Tilda had thought only very rich people could afford such vibrant colours, but here were ordinary-looking Londoners with red tunics and blue dresses. And the clothes were cut differently too. She wore a loose-fitting gown; the girl she could see buying a pie from a street vendor ahead of them wore a dress so tight you could see the narrow curve of her waist and the swell of her hips. It was most disconcerting.

Tilda overheard people say they were expecting a vast human tide from the north and south. The way they spoke she could tell these city people had a low opinion of their country cousins. They were afraid of them, or contemptuous. Would they burn their houses down and murder them? Or would they be able to sell them bread and pies at four times the usual asking price? Looking at those hard, beady faces, Tilda felt a sudden affection for the good-hearted country people she knew. They seemed closer to God and goodness than this greedy lot.

As the houses loomed above them Tilda noticed how the streets grew darker as the upper floors almost touched from either side of the street. And this was still outside the city walls. She guessed it must be even more crowded beyond the river, in the city itself.

The bustle in the streets grew more alarming and she was shoved out of the way by one impatient young man. Her father grabbed him by the scruff of the neck, and made him say he was sorry for his bad manners.

'Not far to go now,' said Thomas, who had once or twice led them in the wrong direction. 'It's been several years since I visited, and the place has changed a fair bit.' But around eight of the clock, and there were certainly many church clocks to chime the hour, they stopped right on the south side of the river, overlooking a great bridge.

'We're here,' said her father. Tilda looked at the house before them. How had her uncle managed to find himself such a palace? she thought. A door – a proper door with hinges and a lock – stood between two large, shuttered windows. And there was a floor above – and even a floor above that. Uncle John lived in a house that had three floors! Their single room in Aylesford seemed even more of a hovel. She wondered how grand her relatives would be. Should she curtsy and call them sir and madam, as you were supposed to do to the lord and lady of the manor?

When her father knocked on the door there was no reply. He knocked again and a voice snarled, 'Who is it?' Tilda was frightened by the violence in the voice but the tone changed when Thomas told him who he was.

The door opened and a younger man, but easily recognisable as a Rolfe, opened the door with a smile. 'My dear brother,' he said. 'Welcome to London town.' He gave Thomas a hug and said,

'We have heard about the revolt. I was hoping you would come!'

They were ushered into the house and the door locked firmly behind them. The family assembled to gawp at them – a suspicious-looking woman and three children all under the age of ten, Tilda guessed. She noticed how they were dressed so much smarter than her and her father. The colours and cloth of their clothes were so much brighter and cleaner. All at once she felt terribly dowdy.

John Rolfe introduced them. 'My wife Alice, and William, Simon and Joan.'

Thomas beamed. 'A pleasure to see you again, Alice. And to meet your lovely children. And this,' he said with a flourish, 'is my dear daughter Tilda.'

Tilda gave a little curtsy and the family smiled politely. The less than warm welcome had made her feel uneasy.

'We heard there was a violent mob coming,' said Alice. 'Are you part of it?'

Thomas told them they had nothing to fear. That they had marched from Aylesford with the rebels and had seen no violence against ordinary people. Only manor houses and records offices had been attacked. The people in the street had nothing to fear from the rebellion.

This seemed to reassure the household. John asked if they had eaten and when they said they were starving hungry his wife produced a half-consumed pork joint and bread and they sat round the table to eat.

'And what of you, Tilda, what is to happen in your future?' asked Alice. 'Is there a boy in Aylesford you have your eyes on?'

Tilda blushed. 'There must be someone who likes the look of you,' teased Alice. 'You're a fine-looking girl, and what I'd give for your head of lovely dark curls.'

'All the boys in our village are muck-spouts and scobber-lotches,' said Tilda, making the children giggle. 'I want to meet a boy who is kind and clever and can teach me how to read.'

Alice looked on with admiration. 'You might have to come to London to find such a rare creature,' she said. 'And maybe settle for one or two of those wonderful virtues rather than all three!'

Thomas laughed. 'Don't you go tempting my Tilda away from Aylesford,' he said. 'I want her to stay only a short distance from her father. She's all I have in the world.'

As they sat and ate their supper, Tilda asked a hundred questions about the mighty city she found herself in. Yes, explained Alice, even though it was over the river from London itself, Southwark seemed to be every bit 'London' as the rest of the place. The houses were just as close together. Southwark was famous for its bath houses, they told her. They were usually right next to the river and a plentiful supply of water.

Tilda liked the sound of that – after the walk to London the idea of soaking in a hot bath seemed like the ultimate luxury. But John rapidly persuaded her that this was a terrible idea. 'They're dens of sin,' he said. 'Full of Flemish ladies who are all too free with their favours.' Tilda sort of knew what he meant and began to blush. She would have to take a bath somewhere else.

Talk of bathing and smelling sweet made Tilda remember the perfume she had stolen. Impulsively, she took the plain glass bottle from the pocket in her skirt and said, 'Auntie Alice, we picked this up on our travels. I thought you might like it.'

Her father began to speak. 'Tilda, this is not a wise...' But John waved at him to be silent.

Alice's eyes lit up and she plucked the bottle from the table and carefully prised off the glass stopper. But after a quick sniff, her face turned stern. 'Tilda, this is a scent from heaven. But I can never wear it. People will know immediately that I have stolen it – as I know that you too must have done. People know immediately when something isn't right for a person. It's the same with the laws concerning clothing... you see a shopkeeper in a fur-lined coat, and you know at once he's stolen it.'

John took the bottle and smelt it. 'It's beautiful.' He smiled. 'Perhaps we'll just keep it for ourselves...'

That awkward moment passed but talk about the imminent arrival of the rebels was never far away.

'We are all God-fearing Christians and loyal to our king,' Thomas said, further seeking to reassure his relatives. 'We have no quarrel with the ordinary people of London. And we will not be looting and rampaging. We have come to talk to the king, to ask him to stop listening to the corrupt counsel of evil men. We want him to stop sending his tax collectors to fleece us and to free us from servitude and allow us to work for a fair wage.'

John looked on with incredulity. 'Well, best of luck with that,' he said.

CHAPTER TEN

June 13, 1381

Tilda woke the next morning to find bright sunlight streaming through the shutters of her attic room. She knew instinctively it was far later than her usual waking time – all that walking must have tired her out. She opened the shutters and peered down at the busy street below. The city, it seemed, was gripped by anxiety. All around, people were putting up boards on their shops and windows, the sound of hammers banging in nails drowning out the usual cacophony of horses' hooves and cartwheels on dirt streets, and the bustle of thousands of people.

The clock struck seven and she listened for any noise inside the house. Everyone else was still asleep so she went back to bed too – something she almost never had the luxury of doing in Aylesford. The evening had ended pleasantly. Tilda had helped Alice clear away and wash the dishes from their meal and then told the children a bedtime story. They had listened intently to the tale about the goose that laid a golden egg. And when they had begged for another she told them about the boy who cried wolf. Her mother had told her these stories when she was tiny and although she could not read herself she had a talent for remembering them.

It was just after she heard the clock strike ten that Tilda became aware of a distant rumbling – feet, voices – an almost invisible presence to begin with, like a storm brewing – that grew louder every minute. Thomas came up to her attic room and they watched the new arrivals swell into the narrow streets, making it impossible to go any way other than into London itself. Tilda felt safe up there and excited to be part of these extraordinary events. She realised she liked the anonymity of London. If she had done anything bad back in

Aylesford someone would have known, someone would have reported her. Tilda was not by nature likely to do anything wicked. But she still liked the idea that here she could go and knock the hat off an archbishop and no one would have a clue who she was. But in enjoying that thought she had a sudden realisation that many among this crowd must be thinking the same thing and that some of them would be prepared to do much, much worse.

'Tilda, look at this,' said her father. 'Some of our crowd have proper weapons. I'll bet we have been joined by soldiers or maybe even runaways from the army.'

'Let's go with them,' said Tilda, anxious to see what would happen next.

'No,' said Thomas firmly, his voice clearly indicating that this was something they were not going to discuss. Tilda was about to raise her voice in protest. But her father said, 'Ahead is the bridge. Its gates will be bolted and the drawbridge pulled up. If we go out now there will be an almighty crush.'

Tilda could see the sense in that. 'So let us wait until the crowd comes to a halt and then decide what to do.'

Over in the Tower, King Richard and his advisors stood in the high ramparts. Guy had been here on only a couple of occasions before and could quite believe it was the safest place in London. The great walls and heavy drawbridge, and the concentrated presence of soldiers, made him feel well protected. This was something to be grateful for, as their circumstances were growing more dangerous by the hour. Messengers had been visiting all morning with alarming news of mass crowds from both Kent and Essex descending on the city.

Southwark was not too far from the Tower and now they could clearly see a great crowd massing on the south bank in the summer sunshine. 'The drawbridge should be up,' said Richard with alarm. 'Send word at once to the gatekeepers.'

But even as he spoke the crowd began to flow across the bridge – too small from that distance to spot individual faces, but easy enough to see en masse. Richard sat down on the floor of the ramparts, quite speechless. Guy thought it an oddly un-king-like posture to adopt. Almost like a cat, sitting resting its back against a wall, back legs splayed apart. Then Richard stood up and looked again. 'Why has my order been disobeyed?' he screamed. He sounded almost tearful.

*

Tilda and Thomas continued to watch from their attic perch. The crowd kept on flowing through Southwark – there must have been thousands of people now arriving into London.

John ran up the stairs to join them. 'The bridge is down and the gates are open!' he shouted excitedly. 'London is on your side, brother.'

Thomas was still cautious. 'Maybe they have deliberately let us across, so the soldiers can attack us when we are tightly packed together.'

John was unconvinced. 'Come on, let's seize the moment,' he said. 'If that was going to happen, it would have happened earlier. There's thousands that have crossed over now.'

The three of them rushed out to join the rebels, although John told his wife and children to stay safe inside the house. Alice didn't argue, obviously fearful of what was to come.

Outside, the crowd continued to funnel into the narrowing streets, like a great tide of water filling the nooks and contours of a rocky beach. Tilda noticed that although most shops were closed and boarded, a few bakers and other vendors of street food were braving the mob. Their bravery had paid off. Most were almost sold out of their loaves and pies and pastries. That was reassuring to Tilda. It seemed to indicate that people weren't going to go mad and rob anything they thought they could. As did the fact that many still carried flags of St George to show their loyalty to the king.

They were swept along to the vast bridge across the Thames, which led into London town itself. 'Look at this, Tilda,' said Thomas. 'I can't believe the bridge is open. I thought they would close the gates as we approached. Is this a trap?'

The bridge was an unbelievable sight. Other than the huge cathedrals, which were so vast and tall Tilda found it impossible to imagine they had been built by mere humans, London Bridge was the most astonishing thing she had ever seen. As well as crossing the wide river in a series of arches, it also had buildings on either side – houses and shops, for heaven's sake. Tilda wondered what it would be like to live in a house overlooking the river. She didn't know whether it would be the most exciting thing in the world or whether she would spend her time wondering when the whole edifice might collapse into the river if there was a terrible storm.

As they passed under the gatehouse she felt grateful that the gatekeepers had decided to let the peasant army in. Those sturdy gates looked like a formidable obstacle. She also noticed a collection of heads on spikes staring sightlessly on the rebels. She shuddered and looked away. Would any of their heads be up there in a few days' time?

'Perhaps King Richard agrees with our cause,' they heard people say. 'Perhaps he is holding back his soldiers.'

As they poured over the bridge, Tilda could see they were being greeted as friends rather than enemies. Londoners flocked out to join them. Some even came with baskets of fresh-baked bread and flagons of ale. On the north side they found there were rebels from Essex, arriving at the same time. As the crowds gathered in the narrow streets, their bodies became increasingly packed together and Tilda began to feel afraid.

'We need a big space to gather,' said Thomas.

They were carried closer to the centre of the city and a large market square. Tilda noticed the mood of the crowd was growing tense. The voices she heard around her were now a mixture of London and country people.

Someone threw a bottle at the upper window of a fine house. As bottle and glass window shattered, everyone cheered. Almost at once Tilda no longer felt part of something good and right. This crowd were sensing their power and the prospect of unleashing their anger on the capital city.

Over the excited conversations that surrounded her, Tilda heard other more alarming noises. There was splintering and crashing and smoke could be seen rising over the rooftops and spires. 'They're breaking into the prisons,' she heard someone shout. 'Come on...'

Some of the crowd gleefully hared off, obviously looking for trouble. Most stayed where they were. She looked at their faces and guessed they felt like her – wondering what on earth they were going to do now they were here.

But there was worse to come.

*

The change of mood in the crowd was frightening. Now people seemed dangerously excited – almost like young children up to gleeful mischief. Maybe it was because they were all packed so tightly together, especially as there seemed to be a great swathe of people coming down from the streets leading north out of London.

'Must be more of the Essex crowd,' said Thomas. 'We've all got here at the same time.'

Tilda noticed a lot of the rebels were drinking ale and wine. She could smell it in the air. She had seen what drink did to people at village fairs and how wild and reckless it made them behave. She was pleased to have her father and his brother there to protect her.

In the distance, over the boisterous noise of the crowd, Tilda continued to hear more disturbing sounds. Smashing of wood and the crackle of flames. Now, over the rooftops, she could see several plumes of black smoke and the smell of burning timber filled the streets.

'I want to go back to Southwark,' she said, suddenly really afraid. Then she stumbled, almost falling to the ground in the crush of people pushing further into the centre of London. Thomas quickly pulled her to her feet then picked her up and carried her on his back – something he had not done for several years. Tilda was a big, strapping girl, and she was quite surprised he could still do this.

'Hold tight, dearing,' Thomas said. They came to a crossroads and one of the streets was almost empty. 'Quickly,' he shouted to them both, and they found a doorway to stop and sit to rest. There was more noise – that smashing of wood and crackling flames.

Tilda could see John was looking white with fear. 'If a fire takes hold and spreads, we'll all be burned alive in the crush,' he said. 'I want to get back home too.'

But the stream of people, densely packed and agitated, continued to pour past them. Another couple of stragglers, both young men from London, took refuge in the next doorway.

'They've attacked the Courts of Justice,' said one of them. 'Broken in they have. And now they're carrying out all this paper and parchment.'

The other said, 'They're setting fire to great piles of them – must be everyone's tax records.' He laughed with savage glee. 'If they don't know who we are and where we live, they won't be able to tax us.'

Thomas asked them if they knew how to get back to Southwark.

'This street's a dead end,' said the younger of the two. 'You just gotta wait for this lot to thin out, then you can go back the way you came along Fleet Street.'

Three others joined them in the side street – a man and his daughters. They seemed to know the other two Londoners and immediately sparked up a conversation. 'They broke into King's Bench,' said the man. 'Set it on fire.'

John looked worried. 'That place has got some ugly, evil people in it,' he said. Tilda and Thomas looked at him for an explanation. 'It's a prison,' he added.

'Yeah? Well, they let them out,' said one of the new arrivals. He gestured at the procession of people still streaming along the top of the street. 'And they'll be in among that lot.'

Tilda began to wonder what she had done, coming here. She had encouraged her father to join the rebels, and now she was feeling guilty. They had certainly not expected this to happen.

The smell of burning seemed to be getting closer. 'Sparks from the prison fire,' said John. He pointed up at a house across the narrow street. 'Look. The roof is smouldering.'

The new arrivals went at once to bang on the door of the house. A worried-looking woman opened an upper window. 'Your roof's on fire!' they shouted.

'Come on,' said John. 'We need to go. No point staying here and getting burned alive.'

CHAPTER ELEVEN

The three of them went to the top of the narrow street. It still seemed impossible to go back the way they had come – there were simply too many people pushing past them along Fleet Street. So they joined the crowd and soon they found themselves swept along to another long street of grand houses.

Tilda was amazed at everything she was seeing. These houses were all made of stone, rather than wood and straw. They were on several levels – three or four at least – with glass windows all the way to the top. And they all looked like they would stand up to any sort of dreadful storm God chose to throw against them. She could barely understand the sort of wealth you would need to build a house like that. But clearly there were many, many people with that sort of wealth in London.

'This is the Strand,' said John. 'I know who lives here. That John of Gaunt.'

Even Tilda and Thomas had heard of him. John of Gaunt was King Richard's uncle, and supposed to be the richest man in England, aside from the king of course. Everyone in Aylesford was convinced that half the taxes they paid went straight into his pocket. He was also Richard's chief general and had led the English army in a succession of failed campaigns in France. If he'd been successful, Tilda once joked, maybe people wouldn't mind him being so rich.

The crowd were collecting around one building that sat squat on the river, a great stone fortress – part castle, part palace, it was easily the grandest building in the street. People were already throwing rocks at the windows and battering on the door. Faces occasionally appeared at upper windows, wide-eyed with fear.

'That's Gaunt's palace,' said John 'They call it the Savoy.'

The entrance to the palace looked formidable – a great wooden door reinforced with sturdy iron bars. 'How are they going to get past that?' said Thomas.

John shrugged. 'Set it on fire?'

But in that day full of surprises came the greatest one yet. The doors began to creak open. Two men sprang out and fled into the crowd. Their action was a clear invitation and the crowd began to pour into the palace.

Tilda and her father and uncle stood amazed as upstairs windows were flung open and brightly coloured clothes were tossed out of them. Then chairs and ornaments began to rain down on the street, causing the crowd outside to back away. But no one ran forward to steal a fine red tunic or a fur-lined cape, nor any of the silver and gold ornaments – instead they began to make great piles of them and set them on fire.

'Come on, let's go and have a look!' said John. Tilda felt reluctant. This was trespassing. This was the sort of crime a peasant would be hanged for, or have their hand cut off. Her father stayed where he was too. 'Come on,' said John, grabbing them both by the arm. 'Let's just have a look.'

They ran through the main doorway into a great courtyard with doors and stairways into the interior. All around, hanging from the walls in massive rooms and halls, were magnificent tapestries. The luxury of the interior made William Laybourne's manor house back in Aylesford look like the humble residence of a provincial clerk. Tilda had never seen anything like it in her life. She was torn between feeling outraged that one man could have so much wealth and humbled by her own ant-like station in the world.

Inside was pandemonium. On the first floor up from the courtyard a great room overlooked the River Thames. The windows here were also open, and groups of peasants were ransacking cupboards full of gold and silver plates and then spinning them out into the river, seeing how far they would skim across the water. Another man was kneeling on the wooden floorboards methodically going through a jewellery box and smashing up the gemstones with a hammer. All around him on the floor were piles of green, red and blue fragments.

There was a mantelpiece containing small gold and jewel-encrusted ornaments, and Tilda picked up an egg-sized paperweight and placed it in the pocket of her skirt. Thomas saw her doing it and grinned. They were both thinking the same thing. We could buy something with that...

Behind them, fierce, angry shouting caught their attention. A group of three burly peasants were dragging a scrawny young man down the stairs. The peasants had a look of grim determination on their faces and the young man looked both bewildered and terrified. 'Let me go. I ain't done nothing!' he shouted.

Tilda and Thomas rushed to the front of the building to see the peasants and their prisoner emerge out on to the street. There were now three large bonfires blazing away. The crowd outside grew silent and one of the peasants announced, 'This man has been caught looting jewellery. We are not here to steal. We are here to send a message to the king and his advisors.'

With that he stabbed the terrified man through the heart and then the three of them cast his lifeless body on to the largest of the bonfires. Tilda watched with mounting horror and felt faint and nauseous as the smell of burning human flesh filled the building. Thomas could see she was about to collapse and came to hold her.

Inside the house, someone near to them pointed directly at her, a corpulent man of middle years with a large wart on the side of his chin. 'That wench stole too,' he said to no one in particular, but loud enough for anyone around to hear him. 'I saw her put a trinket in her gown.'

Tilda took three or four deep breaths then ran to the riverside of the building. Standing by the window she cast the ornament in her pocket as far as she could throw it into the Thames. They watched it sail through the air and land with a small splash in the river.

Thomas towered over the man. 'I'll gladly stab you in the heart if you say another word,' he said. The man shrank before him then ran off down the stairs. Thomas went to join his daughter. 'That could have changed our life,' he said quietly.

Outside they could hear further screaming.

'Have soldiers arrived?' Thomas asked. Tilda felt her legs turn to jelly. Here they were in the house of one of the richest men in England. They had no possible excuse for being there. They would be arrested and executed as sure as night turned to day. They might even be hanged, drawn and quartered.

Tilda looked at the open window over the Thames and wondered whether to take her chances in the river. But it was flowing fast and she was no swimmer. 'If we grab a chair maybe we can throw it in and hold on to that,' she found herself saying. Surely it was better to risk drowning than a grisly public execution?

Thomas rushed to the front of the house and looked out on to the Strand. Another looter had been killed by the rioters. This one had had his head chopped off, the blood now running in rivulets along the cobbled road. His body had been cast on to one of the bonfires and a smell, disconcertingly like roasting pork, wafted up through the windows.

'Don't look,' said Thomas, now white as a sheet. 'But there are no soldiers.'

Tilda didn't like this at all. One minute she was doing something she knew was forbidden, something she had believed her whole life to be bad. But she had been enjoying it, and quite ready to justify her actions to anyone who asked. The next minute she was in mortal fear of torture and execution. All at once she wished she was safe back home in Aylesford.

'Father, I want to get out of here,' she said. 'I don't want to be caught when the soldiers arrive.'

Thomas nodded. 'We'll find John and get back to Southwark. Maybe he's upstairs.'

They ran up a great, wooden staircase but the scene on the next floor up was just as chaotic. Everywhere they looked peasants and Londoners alike were smashing up furniture and ornaments. A few dead bodies lay scattered on the landing. Perhaps they were John of Gaunt's men, guessed Tilda. Servants who had been foolhardy enough to try to protect their master's belongings from the mob.

The next floor up was exactly the same. There were hundreds of people. John could be anywhere. Tilda began to wonder if they could remember how to get back. Then another smell assailed their nostrils. This was coming from inside the house and wafting down the stairs in billowing smoke. The upper floor of the palace was ablaze.

Instinct took over and Tilda and Thomas joined a frenzied dash back to the street. Fortunately, they were among the first to flee and Tilda stood panting hard, trying to get her breath back, watching the crowd emerge from the palace. A strange memory from childhood came back to her – watching a cargo ship at Rochester harbour, which had caught fire. As the small crew gave up fighting the blaze and came to stand on the harbour side to watch as their ship was consumed by flames, so hundreds of rats fled, streaming along the gangplank and scattering the spectators in panic.

Back then, Thomas had picked her up and fled. Now, as she got her breath back, Tilda began to take in the strange, hazy events happening all around her. There was something of a dream in all this. It felt so odd she had to keep asking herself if she was really there. The colours around her – the sunlight on the buildings, the red and black of the flames and smoke, the faces of the rebels – all seemed intense and vivid. Looking about, everything seemed to be happening in a slowed-down kind of way. The noise – the shouting and crackling of flames – all seemed quite distant.

In her oddly detached state, Tilda realised the thing that frightened her the most was people's faces. She couldn't recall another occasion in her life when she had seen this wild abandon, this fierce glee in people's eyes. Maybe it was like this in battle. But that didn't seem right either – in battle you would expect to be killed, surely? So there would be fear mixed in with this savage exhilaration. She was surrounded, she realised, by people who could give in to their basest instincts and not suffer the consequences.

Tilda reached instinctively for her father's arm and realised with sudden panic that he was no longer by her side. Looking all around her she could not see him anywhere.

She wanted to call out, but good sense told her that showing herself to be a panicky, abandoned young girl would be to invite trouble. She put on a brave face and picked up the leg of a chair that had shattered when it had been thrown from a high window. Tilda told herself she was a strong girl and if she looked determined, no one would be foolish enough to threaten her.

A raised, columned porch in front of another grand house stood on the far side of the street and she pushed through the crowd to stand there, to see if she could spot Thomas Rolfe. The porch offered her a good view over the heads of the mob and she understood at once that finding her father in this milling mass of agitated people would be an impossible task. But she did feel safer up there and could take stock of the situation.

Many of these people were Londoners, she guessed, by the cut of their clothes. They certainly didn't look as drab and shabby as the peasants. Their faces too seemed fuller, less weathered and weary. This great crowd really was a mixture of locals and outsiders from the shires, and the Londoners seemed to hate the king and his government just as much as anyone else.

The smell of burning wood was growing intense. The fire in the Savoy Palace had really taken on the top floor, and much of the roof was now ablaze. Tilda could see fire flickering inside the shattered windows of the lower floors too. Soon this great building was going to be a threat to the lives of anyone close by. Even if it didn't collapse, the heat from the flames would be deadly. She had to get to safety...

Tilda's thoughts were snatched back to the present by the cry of a youth. She felt a tugging on her skirt and realised it was him. Tilda looked down at the leering young man, his face contorted by beer and lust, and tried to understand what he was shouting at her. There was so much other noise going on she could barely hear, but she knew enough to be afraid and disgusted. She snatched up her skirt and delivered a quick kick to his face, taking care that the youth should not grab her leather boot.

The young man howled in anguish then fell back, with a look of drunken astonishment. Tilda realised at once she had done something stupid. Were there others with this youth who would retaliate? He was on the floor now, struggling to get up. But she could see that it was the drink that had incapacitated him, rather than her own strength. The youth did have others with him but they were laughing uproariously at his plight. She had been quite forgotten. All the same she cursed her foolishness, lashing out like that.

The crowd milled below her, almost like a choppy sea. The youth and his companions might have forgotten her, but she was starting to notice a lot of men staring at her. It was time to move on. But where should she go? Could she remember her way back?

CHAPTER TWELVE

Back at the Tower the day had not gone well, although Richard had regained his kingly manner and his face was now a mask. The hysteria he had shown on witnessing the bridge crossing had gone but his anger was unmistakable. Guy de Clare had not seen him smile all day. Everything he said was terse, abrupt. Servants especially were being treated with withering contempt and petty violence. When one chamber boy came to him with the wrong shoes, Richard clouted the young lad so hard around the head he burst into tears. That annoyed the king even more and the boy was immediately dismissed from his household.

But what was especially interesting to Guy was the manner of the king's chief advisors – Treasurer Hales and Chancellor Sudbury. Their usual haughtiness, lofty pronouncements and gestures had gone. Now, they circled the king like wary animal keepers, charged with the care and maintenance of an unpredictable lion. They spoke to each other occasionally in hushed whispers and everything Richard said they leaped on to assure him of their loyalty and duty to the crown.

Hales and Sudbury both had that pale doomed look about them. They breathed in shallow breaths, and they constantly seemed to be fighting off an attack of the hiccups, or bad indigestion. Guy knew what was going on. He had seen such behaviour in men due to be sentenced before a court for a capital offence. This was naked fear. And Guy could guess what was going through their minds. He knew the rustics had demanded the heads of the king's advisors. And maybe those very same men knew full well what was going on in their monarch's head. Were their lives a price he was prepared to pay to get these stinking, uneducated scum away from his capital city? Should he trade their lives in the hope that the mob would spare the life of their monarch? It would be a shrewd move, to be sure. The peasants had assured him that their loyalty still lay with their king. But they were seethingly angry at someone – and that someone was plain enough. It was reported they even chanted the names of the men they were certain were responsible for their unhappiness.

*

Sometime after their midday meal, a courier cried in alarm from atop the castle walls. 'Fire by the river. Fire in the Strand.'

Richard stood up at the long dining table and ordered his advisors to stay seated. 'De Clare, come with me,' he snapped at Guy.

There were now several fires around London – they had seen the King's Bench prison set ablaze not long after the peasants had first crossed the river that morning. But this one sounded even more alarming.

The two of them hurried up the winding stone staircase that led to the highest ramparts of the Tower. Looking along the length of the river, just before the great bend, they could see a plume of black snaking into the sky. Red and yellow flames flickered among the dense smoke.

'That must be the Savoy Palace,' said Richard coldly. 'My uncle will be most displeased.' He gave himself a flicker of a smile – one that did not reach his eyes. 'When he returns, he will be the perfect gentleman to teach these rustics their place.'

Guy was still unsure what was expected of him at a time like this. He knew it would be gross impertinence to ask the king for an opinion. But should he offer his own, uninvited? He decided, instead, on observation. 'Look, my lord, there are fires throughout the city too.'

There were too – none as big as the Savoy, but everywhere you turned, from the south-side settlement of Southwark to the western edges around Westminster and further north at Farringdon and Clerkenwell, smoke sent oily fingers into the clear blue sky. Down below, in the narrow streets and passageways, crowds of various sizes milled almost as aimlessly, like mist in a breeze.

Richard looked at Guy with cold disdain. 'Your king has his own eyes to see,' he said. Guy stood stiffly to attention and wondered what on earth he was expected to do. Then Richard put a hand on his shoulder and gave him a friendlier smile. 'Be not so anxious, de Clare.'

Guy hated this side of Richard. One minute he would be lordly and arrogant, the next like a boy in need of a friend. It was so awkward. Guy liked him when he was nice. But it made the times when he was horrible even more unpleasant. Guy could cope with nonstop lordly arrogance. He knew where he was then. But this constant changing was exhausting.

Richard stood right beside him, close enough for their shoulders to be touching. Then he put an arm round Guy's shoulder. 'What a burden, this kingship,' he said with a sigh. 'And what a time the rustics have chosen to descend on our city. We have but six hundred men to defend us. Their loyalty, I think, I can depend on.' He paused and looked at Guy. This was his cue to speak.

'My lord, I have no reason to fear the Tower guard will side with the mob,' said Guy. 'But these two days have brought many surprises.'

Richard nodded. 'Yes, that is my concern too. At this moment, we cannot count on anything.' He looked over the narrow streets and passageways. 'But these crowds, they are not just the rustics from Kent and Essex. There are Londoners among them – surely. There are too many of them just to be peasants arrived from the shires, and some move with a purpose.' He pointed at one swarming mass heading north from the Tower. 'These are not timid newcomers. They know exactly where they are going.' He gestured to another determined mob. 'And I imagine these ones are seeking out the Flemish settlers perhaps?' Richard nodded to himself. 'I would not want to be Flemish on a day like this. There are scores to be settled. They came here as exiles from their own land, but they have proved too good at their weaving trade to be much liked by the Londoners.'

Guy detected a morsel of sympathy in his voice. 'The mob are turning on the outsiders. What can be done to protect them?'

Richard looked pensive. 'They will have to protect themselves,' he said plainly. 'They will have to claim sanctuary in our churches. We cannot spare our own soldiers. Besides, if we send our few guards into the crowds, who can say how many will turn against us? Either from fear of our impossible situation, or because they have had their foolish heads turned by the anarchy around them.'

Hearing these words, Guy felt a rising sense of alarm. If the King of England was in fear of his life, then what chance did he have?

'What to do, what to do?' said Richard. 'The rustics want my lords Hales and Sudbury. Should I give them to them?'

Guy felt the colour drain from his face. He was horrified to be asked such a question. To say yes was plainly treasonable. People had been hanged, drawn and quartered for less.

Richard, sensing Guy's reluctance to offer an opinion, spoke on. 'I feel, in some way, those men are responsible for all this. Perhaps this ignorant rabble are not as ignorant as we assume.'

'My lord, an ignorant mob will never be satisfied. If you give them the two highest courtiers in London, who knows what else they will demand?'

Richard nodded briskly. 'You answer wisely, de Clare. But we have to give them something. Shall we give them you?'

Guy felt his legs start to go beneath him. He had seen men executed and even now, the sight of a man kneeling before the executioner filled him with dread. What final thoughts went through their head at a time like that? Did they fall into oblivion the moment the axe severed their head from their neck, or did they feel the agony of the cut and the sharp crack of their head as it hit the paving stone beneath the block? And even more horrible to contemplate, if their head was immediately impaled on a spike to be held aloft, did they feel that too?

Richard smacked him hard on the back and laughed. 'They would be no more interested in you than any young lad who wears an ermine cloak and a red felt hat.' He laughed – happy for the first time that day. 'Do not worry, Guy de Clare. You are a useful councillor, but we still remain entirely ignorant of how to extract ourselves from this towering folly.'

King Richard and Guy de Clare descended from the Tower ramparts and returned to the court. The courtiers fell immediately silent as they entered the chamber. With all eyes on them, Richard returned to his throne at the far end of the room and sat down upon it, his eyes coolly appraising the assembled noblemen. Each man, Guy noticed, averted his eyes as Richard's gaze settled upon him.

After a minute of uncomfortable silence, Richard spoke. 'Here is what we shall do,' he said in his reedy voice. 'We shall tell the rustics and the London mob that we shall meet them face to face to hear their demands.'

No one spoke. But Guy could sense fear in the room like an eerie vapour. He gave himself a wry smile. Richard had said nothing of this to him. Guy wondered if he had thought of it on his way back to the throne room. Whatever, it was a sound plan – the best they could do in these difficult times.

'My lords Treasurer Hales and Chancellor Sudbury,' demanded the king. 'Present yourself to me.'

The two chief ministers came forward and stood in front of their king. Both looked pale with fear. 'I want you to arrange for messengers to go out to the mob. We need to establish who the leaders are. And we need to tell them that I shall meet them face to face.'

Chancellor Sudbury stood tall. 'I will take a squadron of my best men and establish this at once, Your Majesty,' he said.

Richard gave a half-hearted smile. 'You will do no such thing, my lord. Send the squadron with your most trusted lieutenant, but do not go yourself. It is far too dangerous.'

Treasurer Hales spoke next. 'But Your Majesty, if you go to meet them, will not your life be in equal danger?'

Richard shook his head. 'These rustics proclaim their loyalty to me. They are convinced that others have misled me.' He paused and looked pointedly at his two chief advisors. 'I feel safe enough.

'Now hurry. Have the messengers return by nightfall and tomorrow we shall see what we shall see.'

Silence descended on the court. In the distance, the sound of rampaging mobs and burning buildings continued to filter in through the Tower windows.

CHAPTER THIRTEEN

Tilda tried to keep a grip on the creeping fear rising in her stomach. This was something she seemed to be feeling with an awful regularity. Here she was, alone in a dangerous crowd and a strange city. She was totally lost. She thought again of the leafy byways of Aylesford and the world she knew so well. 'Come on, Matilda,' she said under her breath. 'You can sort yourself out here.'

The river – it was just the other side of the burning palace. The river was where they had crossed over the great bridge from Southwark. The river would be her way home.

Tilda pushed her way back into the crowd, buffeted like a small boat in a storm. She held on to her chair-leg cudgel as if her life depended on it, and it did. At several points edging down the side of the street, pushing through the torrent of people, she felt hands grab her body. She dealt with these fleeting attempts to grope her by a swift pinch.

She had done this several times over the last two years whenever the village had held one of its annual harvest dances. The village boys had been drunk then as well, but they had the whole village watching their behaviour, and no one would do anything too out of the ordinary. This was quite different. Here, as well as the groping hands, she would occasionally be grabbed around the waist and find herself pulled backwards, especially as she crossed little streets leading away from the main one. When this happened, Tilda swung around at once, before her assailant got too firm a grip, and smashed the end of her chair leg into their body. Then she would move away as quickly as she could, not even looking at who had attacked her.

She fought off two or three assaults as she made her way back. But as she did so, she felt more certain that she was beginning to recognise the route. A side street here, a building there. Shops

141

too, or shop signs at least. Unlike the traders who had greeted the rustics when they first arrived, no one was foolish enough to keep their businesses open with a crowd like this on the street.

There was a sign for the Swan inn. She remembered that because Thomas and John had both declared they had a powerful thirst and had been disappointed it was closed. Further down from the inn was a sign for an apothecary – earlier on Tilda had been disappointed to see that closed too. She was fascinated by the smells and strange-shaped bottles she had seen in such shops whenever her father had taken her to a local town.

She repeatedly told herself that if she kept going she would arrive at Uncle John's house soon enough. She couldn't remember exactly where that was, but she was confident it would come back to her when she got there.

The crowd had begun to thin out a little and Tilda breathed easier. There were still sporadic fires along the way but nothing blazed so fiercely as to cause other buildings to catch and build to a great conflagration. As her eyes darted around, seeking further familiar places, she saw something that immediately made her turn around and retch. She had seen such sights before, of course, what other girl or boy had not. Ahead, in the gutter, lay a headless body, a trail of blood colouring the dirt road. The clothing told her it was a man, although she did not want to look close enough to guess his age. The head was nowhere to be seen.

Tilda covered her eyes and hurried past, trying to supress the urge to vomit. But ahead there were more bodies – men and women by the look of it, and even a child. This was turning into a hideous nightmare. Now the noise of an angry mob caught her attention, and screaming and shouting. Panicky voices filled the air. But this was not a language Tilda knew. These were people from another country. She looked either side, hoping to avoid the murderous scene ahead. But away from the main thoroughfare were sinister, dark alleyways. Tilda knew instinctively that these were places a young girl like her would be molested and possibly murdered. She pressed on.

Ahead, a gang of fifteen or so London youths – she could tell at once by their clothes – had cornered a man and a woman. They had both of them pressed against a wall and were holding them by the throat. All the Londoners carried weapons – swords, daggers, even axes – and Tilda could see the people they were attacking looked terrified.

'Say bread and cheese,' shouted one young thug, his face an inch away from the woman.

Tilda could not help herself. 'What have they done?' she said, but everyone ignored her. She began to push her way through the mob. 'What have these people done?' she pleaded. 'They are common people like all of us.'

An older man pushed her roughly to the ground. Her chair leg skittered out of her hand. 'Keep out of this, you witless rustic,' he said. He picked her up by the scruff of the neck, her dress almost choking her, and threw her further on her way.

Tilda did not need to be told twice. She picked up her stick and ran as fast as her legs would carry her, the screams of the poor man and woman, and their desperate pleading in a foreign tongue, echoing in her ears.

CHAPTER FOURTEEN

Tilda saw several more bodies on her search for London Bridge, although she was grateful she did not see anyone else being murdered. Some of them had had their heads cut off. Some of them just lay there covered in blood, with everything intact. It was now early evening and she was becoming very frightened. In this part of London, with its narrow streets and sharp, dark smells, it was getting more and more difficult to recognise and navigate. Once again, she longed for the clear air and open fields of Aylesford.

Up ahead, a building was ablaze. In front of it two young men were tumbling close to the flames in a vicious fight. Others stood around cheering them on, waving flagons of beer and bottles of wine. There were no women among them and Tilda knew in an instant they would make sport of her if she walked past. There were too many dark corners and too much mayhem going on for anyone to notice a country girl being grabbed and dragged away.

Some of the young men were staring at her, though they seemed so drunk she wasn't even sure they were seeing her. But one or two had an insolent leer on their face. Tilda instinctively darted up a side street that seemed to be leading somewhere north – somewhere she knew was away from the river – but she could see it wasn't a dead end, and she thought if she kept her bearings, up for a bit, then turn right, then along, she would surely come back to the great bridge to Southwark, if she turned back down again when she had passed the blazing building.

But this street offered no greater safety. Up here was busy too – people marauding around in small groups, shouting and carousing. They were all men. Tilda longed to see a group of women she could ask for directions or plead with for protection. Whenever she saw a gang heading her way, she would hide in a narrow alley, back pressed firmly against a porch door or in the gaps between the houses. For once, she was glad her clothes were so drab – the brown hessian blended in well with the fading light. Anything white would have stood out in this dingy backstreet world.

Now Tilda could hear angry voices inside the house she squeezed away in. London voices. They too had been drinking. They seemed pretty upset about something. 'Swines taking our jobs.' 'Swines stealing our customers.' There was a woman there too. She seemed to be trying to calm them down. 'You can't break the fourth commandment, John. Put that down. Put that down. Thou shalt not kill...'

There was a scuffle, and screaming. Tilda wondered for a moment if the woman was being murdered. But then the door burst open and three men tumbled out. All of them could barely stand and each carried a weapon of some sort – a sword, an axe, a dagger. Tilda pressed herself as far as she could into the shadows. The three men staggered down the street, heading towards the mayhem she was desperately trying to escape. A woman shot out, shouting hysterically after them. 'Thou shalt not kill. Think of your immortal souls...' She was so incandescent with rage, Tilda did not immediately think to ask her for help.

The door slammed shut and she could hear bolts and boards being drawn and attached. She waited until the men were out of sight then knocked on the door. There was no reply. She knocked again. A frightened female voice called out above her head, 'Who the devil are you? Go away before I get my husband on to you.'

Tilda looked up. A plump white face stared down at her. 'Please, Mrs,' said Tilda. 'I'm trying to stay safe. I've got family in Southwark and I'm completely lost.'

The face disappeared and Tilda hoped for a moment she was coming down to let her in. But she could hear no creek of staircase footsteps. She looked up to see the woman with a wooden pail and instinctively knew what was coming. Tilda darted away as the foul-smelling waste landed with a splat right where she had been standing. She ran further up the street, laughing at her narrow escape, with the curses of the woman ringing in her ears.

Now it was close to twilight and it had become increasingly difficult to see. The street came out to another wider one but Tilda felt alarmed as she realised she could not tell one way from another. The streets all had the same ramshackle houses, the same shop signs, the same dirt and debris.

She looked left and right – this way at least was deserted. Remembering her plan, she darted right down the dirt road, keeping to the darkest shadows and hoping she would not run into any trouble. The more she ran the more she realised she was getting hopelessly lost. Behind, she could hear a scuffle and screams echoing along the empty street. Again, that awful sound of incomprehensible, terrified cries. She knew someone was calling for help, even if the words were meaningless. She thought of the men who had spilled from the house just now and shuddered at what they might be up to.

Running away from the screaming, she turned a corner and ran right into a scene from a nightmare.

Three dead bodies lying in the middle of the street with a small child crying hopelessly in the midst of them. Tilda did not stop to think. She picked up the child and carried him back to the shadows.

'Who are you?' she said, looking into the face of a boy who could not be more than five or six. He looked terrified and spat full in her face. Instinctively, she dropped him and he ran off. Tilda wiped the spit off with her sleeve and called after him, 'Come back, you silly boy. I want to help you.' But he hurried round a corner and was gone.

Straight ahead, there was another bunch of young men, blades of every description hanging by their sides and glinting in the flames of a street bonfire. Tilda turned and ran again, this time into a narrow alley. At the end there was a blank wall. If they came down here looking for her she would have nowhere to escape.

Tilda pressed herself into a hollow by the side of a house and hoped her breathless gasping wouldn't give her away. Thank heavens this was not the season for breath you could see escaping from your mouth. She could hear them approaching and strained against every urge to peer from her hiding place to see if they were coming her way. Drunken voices grew louder, then, she dared to hope, perhaps fainter. She let a long sigh of relief escape from her lips just as a hand encircled her waist and pulled tightly.

CHAPTER FIFTEEN

Tilda dropped her chair leg as she was pulled back into the alley and began to wriggle like an angry cat. But instead of a lecherous male voice she realised a young woman was speaking to her. The voice was pleading, 'Pleash, to help me.' The accent was a foreign one. She sounded like the people Tilda had seen being attacked earlier.

'Let me go,' hissed Tilda. The arm around her waist loosened its grip. Tilda braced herself ready to run as fast as she could. But the voice spoke again, on the brink of tears. 'Zey kill my friend, in front everybody. No one help.'

Realising she was alone with this stranger, Tilda turned around and peered into the gloom. Her assailant was a small woman a little older than her – perhaps twenty years of age – and obviously not a threat. She was also bruised and bloodied. She wore a white smock, stained red from a wound on her shoulder, and torn on the sleeve.

Tilda held up her hands to show she was not carrying a weapon. 'How can *I* help you?' she said, speaking slowly to ensure she was understood. 'I am from the countryside and I don't know my way around here.'

The woman stared at her, lost for words. Tilda put a hand on her uninjured arm and pulled her further into the alley. 'Let's hide down here, and wait for sunrise.'

'Zo you not kill me?' said the woman.

Tilda suppressed a snigger. She was feeling light-headed with exhaustion but also relief that she had not been grabbed by a gang of drunken men. 'Why would I do that?' she replied.

The woman could barely contain her anger. 'Ve liff here ten year – I come here as gurl. Now people turn against. People ve lend money. People ve give present. People ve look after young children.'

Tilda shook her head. She was feeling bewildered. At the end of the alley was a low wall and beyond that was a larger house with a garden. The wall had dense vegetation nestling up against it. 'Here is a good place to hide,' said Tilda. 'Do you think?'

They climbed over the wall and hid beneath the bushes. In the house a dog started barking but its owners angrily shut it up. Tilda feared they would let it out into the garden to sniff them out. The woman could read her thoughts and reassured her. 'Zey keep dog with zem,' she said. 'In case any break in houze.'

They lay there in the dark, the only immediate sound their shallow breathing, but in the distance fires crackled and people were shouting. Every now and then, screams pierced the air and they both shuddered in horror.

Tilda felt tongue-tied and struggled to think of something to say. The obvious occurred to her. 'I'm Tilda,' she said. 'I live in Aylesford.'

The woman nodded. 'I go zere. Five years ago. Buy wool.' Then she said, 'I am Catherine.'

Tilda tried not to laugh. 'My squirrel's called Catherine,' she said.

The woman gave her a weary smile and shook her head.

'You speak English though, don't you,' said Tilda. 'You can understand everything I say?'

'Yes, but I sound like a Dutch, or a Flemich, whatever you vant to call us. I understand most but I schpeak poor.'

Tilda reassured her. 'No – you're a lot cleverer than I am. I can't speak any other tongues – can't even read and write.'

Catherine smiled. 'You are brave and kind,' she said. 'More important.'

'So what happened?' asked Tilda.

'We walk out shopping for my father. Me and my friend Agnes, she live next door, come down to market, vere there is always good-quality wool. And ze best bread. And we see all this –'she paused – '*commotie*... what is your word? Commotion. And we see all the rustics, all the country people, but a lot of London too. And these men, all drunk and angry, grabbing people, asking them to say 'bread and cheese'. Well those words difficult for Flemish people and when we say wrong they know we not London people.'

Tilda had seen this with her own eyes.

'They grab us both and hold us against wall. They punch me and rip my clothes. I think they will... *verkrachting*... you say rape? I break free and try to help Agnes, but they throw me to ground and I see them...' She ran a hand across her throat. She could barely say the words. 'They kill her. So I run fast and hide. Then you come and help.'

Tilda did not know what to say. She realised in an instant that by coming to London they had stirred up events they had never intended. Anarchy had been let loose on the streets. 'I am so sorry, Catherine,' she said and put an arm round her. Catherine cried softly into her sleeve. It felt odd for Tilda, comforting someone who was older than her. But she was pleased to have met the girl and it made her feel proud of herself, to be able to offer someone protection.

The night air was warm and smoky. Within minutes they were both asleep. But later on they were disturbed by jubilant, drunken voices. London youths, judging by their voices, boasting about their night of murder and mayhem. They were just on the other side of the wall.

'We got three of them on Threadneedle Street,' said one. 'You shoulda heard them squeal.'

'They done a whole bunch of them at St Martin's in the Vintry,' said another. 'Weasels had hidden in the church so they dragged them out. Killed all thirty-five of 'em! Off with their heads! The ground turned red.'

They all found that uproariously funny.

'Serve them right, coming over here, taking our jobs,' said a third. 'They should go back to their own country.'

Tilda could see Catherine's face – the white of her eyes pale in the moonlight. She had never seen such a look of horror on a girl before. She could feel her friend welling up, and prayed she would not start to sob. These boys were clearly up for more murder, and if they heard them they would probably kill them both once they'd asked Catherine to say 'bread and cheese'.

'Jeffrey's lot are heading for Bread Street to see what they can find,' said another voice. 'He's got Godwin with him. Them rustics bust into King's

Bench and let him out. Didn't think we'd see him again until they hanged him at Tyburn. He'll be out there doing some damage!'

'Here, that Godwin. Is he the one who killed that wench when she wouldn't marry him?'

They all laughed, although why it was funny was beyond Tilda.

'Yeah, thasshim,' said one of them. He sounded so drunk it was a marvel he could stand up. 'Silly mare. Mind you, I wouldn't let him near *my* sister...'

They raced off. And Catherine let out a great sob. Tilda hugged her as she cried. 'We're not all like that,' she said.

'I am chure they weavers – appretiches,' said Catherine, when she had managed to stop sobbing. 'They say we take work from them.' She let out a sad sigh. 'We are good at our jobs, but that no reason to kill us.'

Exhaustion overtook them and once again they slept.

*

'Look what we've got here!' A harsh voice caused Tilda to start. She opened her eyes to see three men staring at her and Catherine. One was considerably older and Tilda guessed he was the householder with his two sons. They all had swords and they were pointing them half-heartedly at them. A small dog stood obediently by their side. It looked at them attentively, but it was not growling or baring its teeth.

'Trespassers,' said the eldest man.

'Oh no, sir,' said Tilda. 'We are hiding from the mob.' She spoke to them in the same guarded and respectful way she usually spoke to Lord Laybourne back in Aylesford.

One of the younger men parted a branch that partly hid Catherine from view. 'You've been in the wars,' he said to her. There was a hint of sympathy in his voice.

'My friend has been attacked,' said Tilda. 'She is so shocked she cannot speak.'

The men nodded. 'You are from the country, aren't you,' said the oldest to Tilda, his voice rising in anger. 'You have bought pandemonium to our city.'

Tilda said nothing. She was not going to argue. Help came from one of the sons. 'Come, Father,' he said. 'A lot of the trouble's been caused by our own Londoners.'

There was an ominous pause and Tilda wondered what would happen next.

The older man said, 'It's quietened down now. You best be off.'

It was all the encouragement they needed. 'Thank you, sirs,' said Tilda as they climbed back over the wall.

They hurried along the alley, Catherine holding on to Tilda's arm. 'Zank you,' she said. 'I not need to schpeak.'

'I think they were decent people,' said Tilda. 'I don't think they were ready to attack you.'

Catherine shrugged. 'You have good Englisch saying – "World Turned Upside Down" – who know what they do.'

Out on the wider streets, the morning sun lit the rooftops and chimneys and made the church steeples glow gold against the blue sky. It was colder now, in those first minutes of the dawn.

The streets were almost deserted, although prone figures lay here and there.

'Drunk?' said Tilda.

'Or dead,' said Catherine.

'Do you know how to get to Southwark from here?' asked Tilda.

Catherine nodded. 'Yes. Near here.'

'Where do you live?' asked Tilda, ashamed that she had not thought to ask sooner.

'We have house in Farringdon. It's long way from here, on norz edge of London.'

Catherine looked fearful and Tilda could tell she was frightened to go back on her own. 'You come back with me to Southwark now,' said Tilda. 'And then, when we've had a rest and cleaned ourselves up, we'll take you back to Farringdon.'

Catherine nodded. That seemed to be a good plan.

CHAPTER SIXTEEN

June 14, 1381

Guy de Clare woke early and for a moment he wondered where he was. Since joining Richard's court he had never travelled so much in his life. Windsor one day, the Tower of London the next, or any one of Richard's other residences around the country. Some days he had to look out of the window to remind himself where he was.

He wondered if he would prefer waking up in the same room every day at his parents' Gloucestershire manor house and decided he would now find that crushingly boring. Then he remembered he was in the middle of a terrifying revolt and there were thousands of peasants roaming round outside the castle walls and that everyone at the court was in so much danger there was a chance none of them would still be alive by sunset.

'Master de Clare,' a voice was calling. Guy opened his eyes to see one of Richard's chamber boys standing over his bed. 'His Majesty requests your presence over breakfast.'

Guy got up to splash his face and armpits with water from the bowl by his bed. He didn't want to stink like a rustic in front of the king. The chamber boy took him to an anteroom where the king was already at table, feasting on white wheat bread, eggs and bacon. 'Fetch breakfast for my friend,' he called to no one in particular.

Richard seemed in good humour. He leaned forward and spoke in a conspiratorial whisper. 'We wonder if my lord Sudbury is still with us, or whether he sneaked away in the night. We didn't let him go out yesterday, when he volunteered to speak to the mob. We think he would have headed away from London as fast as his horse could carry his considerable weight.'

Guy allowed himself a tight smile. He never knew what to say to Richard. 'Let us hope the marauding rustics have quietened down, my lord. Perhaps they will all have thick heads from their drinking and today will be much quieter.'

'It is calm on the streets, we hear,' said Richard. 'We have sent word out to the rebels that we shall meet them to discuss their demands.'

Guy looked at the plate of eggs and bacon that had been placed before him and all at once he lost his appetite. 'Is that a safe thing to do, Your Majesty?' he asked.

Richard dropped his devil-may-care manner and looked concerned. 'Who knows, de Clare. Who knows. But we have to do something. We cannot wait here until the mob breaks down the gates of the Tower and drags us all out to be beheaded like criminals. We have heard there is a large group of peasants camped out at Mile End. We shall go there with a small band of soldiers and some of our best advisors and see what we can do.'

Guy wondered if Richard meant Guy too. He thought it best to assume that he did.

'Yes, come on and eat your breakfast,' said the king. 'We have a busy day today. You must record carefully everything that is said. Today we will be making history.'

Guy ate as fast as he could, then begged the king gracious permission to retire and prepare himself for the day. He spent the next half hour sitting on a commode, his guts in turmoil.

*

King Richard II, Guy de Clare, and a small party of advisors and soldiers rode out on horseback from the Tower at eleven o'clock that morning, the clip clop of their hooves and the jingle of buckles and armour echoing around the streets. Lord Chancellor Sudbury and Lord Treasurer Hales were not among them. Richard had decided the sight of those men would only inflame the mob and their place would be to await the return of the royal party.

De Clare did not like either man – each was too arrogant to inspire affection. But he felt a whisper of pity for them, having to while away the day wondering whether their king would decide their heads were the price he was prepared to pay for peace and order to be restored to his capital city.

Riding away from the Tower, Guy noticed that Richard looked especially resplendent in an embroidered cape and golden crown. Despite his young age he was the very picture of kingly magnificence.

Evidence of the night's commotions filled the streets of London and the smell of burning wood hung in the air. Small fires yet to be extinguished still smouldered, occasionally spluttering into flame. Dead bodies, some with heads detached from shoulders, were everywhere. Guy tried not to notice the headless corpses. He felt sick and terrified quite enough.

The journey was punctuated by unexpected exchanges with the ordinary people of London. In previous times the common folk had bowed or cheered upon seeing their king. Now they stared sullenly, and a few impertinent ones, a safe distance from the reach of mounted soldiers and their swords, even shouted abuse. But no one attacked them and no one threw missiles.

Mile End was a twenty-minute ride away and the closer they got the more they sensed a huge crowd lay ahead. It was almost as if the very particles in the atmosphere changed as they approached. The sour air seemed to hum with a malevolent energy and Guy's fear of what lay ahead sat tight around his chest.

As they approached the city walls that bordered an immense field, the size of the crowd took their breath away. Guy had never seen so many people in his life – there were even more people here than on the riverbank at Greenwich. He could not bring himself to believe that there were this many people in England. All at once he feared for Richard and his small entourage. And if Richard's life was in danger, then surely so was his. He looked at the king and was heartened to see he was showing no fear. Instead, he looked entirely inscrutable. Like a hawk about to pounce on prey.

Richard's appearance prompted a strange hush among the crowd. Their silence hung almost like a physical presence over the field. The captain of the guards spoke to the royal party. 'Good God, there must be thirty thousand people here. I have not seen such a number since the Battle of Poitiers.'

Guy felt the gaze of that thirty thousand and it weighed heavily upon him. He realised that if the crowd decided to kill them, they would have no chance of surviving.

The captain said quietly, 'We must ensure we are not encircled. Instruct the rustics to remain where they are and to send their envoys out to speak to us.'

A rider was despatched with instructions that the rebels were not to approach the royal party other than in a single small group.

The city walls and narrow streets were seconds away on a galloping horse. Guy was grateful for the presence of cool-headed, professional soldiers. He kept an occasional eye on what was going on between them and the walls – but no one stood between their line of escape. It did not look like they were being lured into a trap.

The crowd remained silent and continued to stare. It was almost as if those thirty thousand rebels were all holding their breath. None of Richard's party spoke either. All looked wary. This was not the time for small talk. Occasionally a gust of wind blew from east to west, carrying the sweat and stale-dishcloth aroma of the huge crowd. It was a particularly unpleasant smell and proof to

Guy, if any more was needed, of the malevolence of the crowd.

A squawking flock of birds circled overhead, transfixed by this extraordinary gathering of people. In the distance dogs barked and occasional cries could be heard – not of distress, as had happened throughout the night, but of workmen going about their usual noisy business, or a child bawling for its mother.

After an interlude, a small party emerged from the crowd – four rebels on horseback. That intrigued Guy. Plainly there were persons of quality among the rustics here. No peasant would have his own horse, but these men did. He eyed them warily as they approached.

'Do any of you know these men?' said Richard. No one did.

The approaching horsemen stopped within speaking distance, clearly anxious not to allow themselves to be murdered by the king's men.

'Your Majesty, do you assure us of safe passage?' enquired one of the horsemen. He was dressed in a handsome red tunic with a matching velvet hat – the sort of clothes a respectable merchant or some other such guildsman would wear. His voice also indicated refinement and education. This was no common rustic they were dealing with. The others with him looked like overseers or clerks. Clearly they were men who worked with their brains rather than their hands.

'You are safe as long as your companions do not endanger our party,' said Richard. His voice was stern, bordering on threatening.

The four rebels moved a little closer, so they could converse without shouting. The merchant reached for a scroll in a bag on his saddle. 'My lords,' he said, addressing the whole party. 'I have a list of four demands to make.'

Guy was watching Richard closely. He flinched when the man said 'demands' but he did not speak.

Greeted by silence the man looked unsure what to do. Richard smiled and lifted a hand. 'Continue,' he said.

Then he turned to Guy. 'Be sure you record every word.' Guy hurriedly reached for parchment and a pallet, and quill and ink. He had been so transfixed by events he had entirely forgotten why he was there.

The man opened his scroll and spoke in a loud, clear voice. He was obviously someone used to addressing large gatherings of people.

'My lords, we call for the end of bonded labour. Our countrymen should be free to work for anyone they chose for themselves.'

Guy scribbled furiously. Good God, he thought to himself. These rebels are calling for the end of serfdom. How will the country hold itself together if the lord of the manor cannot keep his serfs? There will be anarchy. People will starve.

The man continued. The vast sea of people behind him stayed silent, obviously straining to hear every word.

'We call for the common people to be able to sell the fruits of the labours as they chose, and not to have to give tribute to their lord.'

Guy bristled at this. Why should peasants be allowed to do this? he thought. The lord owned them and the land they farmed on – so the lord owned the things that grew upon it. Why did they think they owed the lord nothing?

All the while Richard remained silent. The man was expecting a response and paused to wait.

'Continue,' said the king.

'We call for land rent to be reduced to four pence an acre, all across the country. No one should be expected to pay more for the land they farm for themselves.'

Guy could not believe his ears. Surely the king would not agree to this. His father had servants to provide for, houses to maintain, and fine clothes cost good money. These things did not come cheap. This rabble wanted something for nothing, or very little. It was the worst kind of treason.

Richard nodded.

'Finally, we call for an assurance that no one shall be punished for participating in this demonstration of our discontent.'

'I have heard and understood you,' said the king. 'And I agree to all your demands.'

Guy could barely contain his astonishment. The world around him would change in an instant if this were true. The lords and ladies would be reduced to the rank of common people. Who then would put food in their bellies, and wood on their fires? Would they be expected to give up their grand houses and their legions of servants? Surely the king could not be agreeing to such treason?

The four peasant representatives looked astonished too. They withdrew out of earshot and hurriedly conferred. The man who had spoken before rode back close to the king's party. 'My lord, we ask that you agree to these demands in writing and also give an assurance in writing that no one shall be punished. We also ask that a charter ensuring these new rights shall be sent to all villages represented here today.'

'We shall instruct our scribes to prepare such documents forthwith,' said Richard.

The four men lowered their heads and rode back to the great crowd behind them. The one who had read those demands to them then spoke as loudly as he could to the rebels. A huge cheer erupted, so deafening it startled all the king's horses, so much so that Guy was nearly thrown off his own. His pen and ink and parchment felt to the ground and he had to rapidly dismount to gather the tools of his profession.

Richard looked on with disapproval. Then he turned to the captain and said, 'We will wait for a moment and then we shall return to the Tower.'

Guy peered at the four horsemen, who had now dismounted and were conversing with a stocky fellow who seemed to be arguing very forcibly with them. Was this, he wondered, the real leader of this mob? He looked like a soldier, certainly someone who could fight. Now the men were getting on their horses again. Moments later they were back speaking to the king.

'Your Majesty,' said their spokesman. 'We thank you for your understanding.' Here he paused, as if uncertain of what he was about to say. Richard stared, inscrutable as ever. 'But we have one more demand to make,' said the man. 'We understand that the chief architects of our woes and unjust oppression have been Lord Chancellor Sudbury and Lord Treasurer Hales. We demand that they should be handed over to us to face their just punishment.'

Guy could not believe his ears. Clearly these rebels were drunk on power. The king's acquiescence had been a terrible mistake. Where would it all end? Richard's reply shocked him even more.

The king thought for a moment then spoke clearly. 'I understand your position. I can assure you that my lords Hales and Sudbury will face justice.'

That seemed to satisfy the men. They rode off back to the crowd, shouting the king's reply before they had even reached the front of the crowd. Another huge cheer sent birds flying from the trees around the field.

'Enough for now,' said Richard. 'Let us leave before they start to ask us if they may live in our castles and manor houses.'

The party turned and began a hasty retreat back to the safety of the Tower.

CHAPTER SEVENTEEN

Catherine knew these streets and just as she had predicted they were back at London Bridge in minutes. 'I'm so pleased you're here,' said Tilda. 'I'd be completely lost without you.' She was beginning to feel she had met someone she really liked.

'Who are you staying with?' asked Catherine. She sounded wary.

'My uncle and his family. They're nice people.'

'And what do they think of us Flemish?'

Tilda had no idea. She shrugged. 'I honestly can't say. We never talked about it.'

'They hate us because we make cloth,' said Catherine. 'We are good at make cloth.'

Tilda was puzzled by this. She knew weavers in Aylesford – didn't everyone? But she had never heard them say anything ill about Flemish people. Evidently the London weavers thought differently. 'My uncle is a builder. I can't imagine he'll have any reason to do you harm.'

The bridge was as busy as ever, and now a few shops along its length had opened for business. Evidently, the urge to make a profit from this huge influx of hungry peasants had overcome the fear of disorder. As they walked past a bakery stall on the bridge the smell of freshly made loaves and biscuits made Tilda weak with hunger and she remembered she had some coins in her purse. 'Let's buy something to take home – some gingerbreads.'

Catherine nodded. Now they were surrounded by people, she didn't dare open her mouth in case they realised she was a foreigner.

The shopkeeper was friendly and asked Tilda for two pennies, which she had, although she thought that was very expensive. In Aylesford four gingerbread biscuits would be half a penny. The man turned to Catherine. 'You've been in the wars, my dearing,' he said. 'Are you all right?'

Tilda said, 'She's been badly mistreated, sir, and has lost the power of speech.'

The man looked puzzled, then suspicious. They hurried away. Catherine whispered, 'Never pay more than penny for gingerbreads.'

Now she was back in Southwark, Tilda began to recognise buildings and streets and it wasn't long before they were back at John Rolfe's house.

Tilda rapped on the door. 'Who is it?' came an angry voice. That was Alice, John's wife.

'It's me, Tilda,' she cried.

The door flew open. Alice gave her a big hug. 'Where have you BEEN?!' she demanded. Tilda realised her auntie couldn't decide whether to be angry or delighted. 'Your father and John are scouring the streets, looking for you. They've been out since daybreak with our William.'

The two younger children, Simon and Joan, peered anxiously around their mother's skirts. 'And who is this?' asked Alice, looking suspiciously at Catherine. 'You've been in a battle or two.'

'This is my friend Catherine,' said Tilda proudly. 'She helped me find my way back here.

I got separated from Thomas and John when they burned the Savoy Palace.'

'Yes, they told me about that,' said Alice. 'They thought you would just head for home. But it's easy to get lost in a strange town, especially one as big as this one. Those streets are a maze. Thank God you are safe.'

Alice turned to Catherine and said, 'We are very grateful to you, my dear. You can get off home yourself now.'

'She's been attacked and nearly killed,' said Tilda swiftly. She decided she would have to tell the truth about her. 'Catherine is Flemish. The mob have been killing Flemish people all over London.'

Alice looked wide-eyed with horror. 'I heard rumours but I didn't believe them, although your dad and John saw a few nasty incidents.' She looked at Catherine. 'I'm afraid you can't come in here, dearing.'

Tilda looked at Alice with astonishment. 'Why not?'

'We've got neighbours who are weavers. They hate the Flemings. "Coming over here taking

179

our jobs..."' Tilda could tell Alice didn't like her neighbours by the way she imitated them. 'But if they knew we were sheltering a Flemish, they'd burn our house down.'

Tilda spoke firmly. 'Aunt Alice, if you will not let her stay I will walk her home to Farringdon.'

'FARRINGDON?' said Alice. 'By God's nails, that's miles away.'

'Please, Auntie Alice,' pleaded Tilda. 'We'll go there when my father gets back.'

Alice shook her head. 'Very well.' The hostility seemed to drain out of her. She decided then and there to be nice and took Catherine by the arm. 'You poor thing,' she said. 'But we'll have to keep you out of sight.'

Catherine was made to sit away from the window in the kitchen but Alice did give her bread and cheese, and milk to drink. Tilda bought her a bowl of water to wash in and asked Alice for a needle and thread to repair her smock.

Just after the church clock struck eleven there was a distinctive rapping at the door. 'They're back,' shouted Alice and rushed to let John, Thomas and William in.

When Tilda ran to greet him, she saw her father was close to tears. 'My dear daughter,' he said. 'I've been so worried. And outside – in the streets... every time we saw the body of a young woman I thought it was you. There are so many of them.' He sat down and covered his face with his hands. 'My God, we should never have come here. Who would have thought our journey would cause so much misery.'

Tilda wished she had never persuaded her father to come, and felt terribly guilty. She changed the subject. 'I'm sorry, Father. I lost you by the palace. I looked around and you were gone. But I found a friend who showed me how to get back here. This is Catherine.'

Catherine emerged from the kitchen. Before she could say anything Alice spoke. 'She's Flemish. We can't let her stay here. The neighbours might turn on us too.'

'Thank you, Catherine,' said Thomas. Then with a nod to Alice, he said, 'We must get you back home immediately.'

They ate a hurried meal of barley bread and cheese then headed off before midday to return Catherine to Farringdon.

John insisted on coming too. 'Can't have you getting lost again,' he said. Tilda was so grateful and relieved that her relatives had decided to help her new friend. They were good people, like her own father.

But shortly after they crossed the bridge they realised the atmosphere on the streets was just as fetid as it had been the day before. Gangs of prowling young men, obviously looking for trouble, jostled past them. When their paths crossed, they would speak to Tilda and her companions and John would always answer them in a friendly way, making it plain he was a Londoner like them, and they should have no quarrel with them.

When she wasn't wondering what the next encounter with a hostile stranger might bring, Tilda marvelled at the variety of the houses and shops and businesses all around her. Most traders had dared to open their shopfronts today and the streets they passed were full of fabrics, spices, leather goods, bread and cakes... If she had the money, she would have stopped and bought something at every one of them.

There were businesses here too, side by side with ordinary dwellings. The sharp, metallic tang of a blacksmith's, the bloody stench of a butcher's... everywhere people were making and selling and struggling and striving to make their living. It was overwhelming but exciting. Everything about London said 'opportunity'. It was the complete opposite of Aylesford... Harrowing and ploughing fields, then marriage to some oafish village lad, and endless days with suckling children, if she didn't die in childbirth. The city, crowded, violent and stinking though it was, offered endless possibilities. Here, the future was unwritten. Tilda realised living in Aylesford was never going to make her happy, especially now, when she had seen a glimpse of a different life.

The further they got from the centre of the city, the further they felt away from danger, although on the edges were the poorest houses. The beggars they had seen when they first arrived, especially the starving children, were much in evidence. But the people here seemed too weak, too listless, to be a threat. Tilda peered down narrow, squalid alleys. She thought the ramshackle hovels, with their cracked tiles and rotten wooden frames, made their own hut back in Aylesford look like the height of luxury. There was something about this part of London that made her think of an animal corpse, its body stuffed with wriggling maggots. It stank just as bad too. Clearly, there were advantages in village life, after all.

Catherine began to look less anxious as they approached streets she knew well.

'I am living here,' she said, pointing to a stone and timber house, its front painted in the black and white style. It was quite substantial – one that a successful merchant would own.

Catherine knocked on the door and a window opened on the first floor. A woman shrieked with joy and ran down the stairs. The door burst open and she covered Catherine with kisses. Both spoke rapidly in a language Tilda assumed was Flemish, and John, Thomas and Tilda stood on the doorstep feeling awkward. Then Catherine remembered who was with her and insisted all three of them come inside. The woman, obviously her mother, spoke. Her English was better although she still had a thick Flemish accent.

'Zis is terrible news. Our friend Agnes, killed by a mob. We dare not go out vile all this is happening,' she said. 'But we are lucky. Our neighbours, they are good English people. They have gone to buy us bread and cheese and oats so we can eat. The world has gone crazy.'

*

Guy de Clare felt safer the further they rode away from the vast mob at Mile End. The narrow streets closed around them and the whole party seemed visibly more relaxed, although the captain of the guard reminded them to be vigilant until they were once again back within the safety of the Tower.

Richard said nothing and his entourage took that as a cue to do the same. He seemed perfectly calm though, perhaps even rather pleased with himself. Guy was full of questions he knew he could never ask. 'Did you really mean it when you said you'd grant them all their freedom from serfdom and that Hales and Sudbury would face justice?' But he knew well enough that this was presumptuous and asking might well see him returned to

Gloucestershire in disgrace. He would have to wait and see what Richard was prepared to share with him later in the day.

But as they approached Whitechapel a messenger from the Tower approached at speed. He spoke with urgency to the captain of the guard who had rode out to meet him. The captain held up his hand to halt the royal entourage and spoke firmly. 'Your Majesty, the Tower is no longer a safe place. We must travel in haste to Blackfriars and take refuge there.'

Richard looked alarmed. Guy could tell by the way his air of smugness had evaporated and his eyes were darting to and fro. 'Ah, the Wardrobe,' he said, trying and failing to sound nonchalant. That was the nickname they gave to this royal storeroom for clothes and armour. 'Captain, when we get there, we command you to go at once to the Tower and report on the situation.'

Guy could sympathise with Richard. He was consumed with fear. The Tower – that royal stronghold with six hundred soldiers to protect them all – had fallen to the rebels. How on earth had it happened? And if the Tower was not safe, then where in London was?

CHAPTER EIGHTEEN

The walk back from Farringdon to Southwark was an exhausting one. Now free of the danger of being accosted with a hated Fleming, and full from the food and drink they had been given by Catherine's family, Tilda, Thomas and John all felt weary.

But as they tramped back in silence Tilda began to feel happier than she had been since they first arrived. When they'd left the Flemish house, Catherine had hugged her and told her to come back and visit her. 'You teasch me schpeak better Englisch. I tcasch you reading and writing!' she had promised.

Tilda felt she had made a real friend. And she had discovered that her uncle John's family were brave, decent people. They weren't the sort of Londoners who would go around killing foreigners, at least. London, she was learning, was full of good and bad people.

She wondered how many of those who had gone out murdering and raping had been prisoners released from the jails. She hoped in her bones that the violence they had witnessed had passed and order would return to their lives. Walking through the city streets now though, she felt great excitement and curiosity. Now, for the first time, she began to seriously consider whether she should stay here and escape from the life that had been mapped out for her in Aylesford.

But nothing was simple. Firstly, she was Lord Laybourne's property and he would forbid her to move. Secondly, her father would be heartbroken if she left him alone in the village. He would surely find another wife, but who knew whether they would love each other as he had loved her mother, and no matter what happened she knew he would miss his daughter terribly. Thirdly, was she cut out to be a London girl? Wouldn't she forever be a simple country bumpkin always to be charged more than double for bread or biscuits?

And those were just the simple problems. The ones she would have faced before this whole upheaval. They all paled into insignificance next to the vexed question of whether the Coopers had seen her and her father take part in the ransacking of Laybourne's manor house. If he came back to Aylesford, he would be keen to take his revenge. Returning home could mean they would end up hanging from a tree.

Tilda's troubled thoughts were interrupted by Uncle John. He held up a hand to stop them. 'Listen,' he said. 'Something's going on up ahead.'

Sure enough, there in the distance they could hear shouting and screaming. And the familiar smell of burning filled their nostrils.

'What shall we do?' asked Thomas. 'We can only get home across the bridge.'

John shook his head. 'We should be all right. We're English. No one has any reason to attack us.'

Close to the river, they could see a great commotion further along to the east, around the Tower, which gleamed white in the summer sunshine. But as they turned into one of the wider streets that approached London Bridge a large crowd milled towards them. They were chanting and shouting and seemed dangerously excited.

As they grew closer, Tilda could see two of the marchers at the front of the crowd were carrying poles with heads jammed on them. She felt sick. 'What would someone do something like that for?' she asked. The three of them hurried into a side street to let this grisly procession pass.

When the crowd thinned out, they continued on their way, but someone was rushing towards them, face flushed, eyes wide and shining. 'It's my neighbour, Robert,' said John. 'He's one of them that don't like the Flemings.'

The man had the appearance of an overexcited child, desperate to share a great story with them. 'We've all been in the Tower!' he said.

'We wondered what was happening there,' said John.

'Yes, we all gathered outside – half of London it must have been. And we all started demanding that the king come out to talk to us. But he wasn't there. He'd gone to Mile End to meet the Essex rebels.

So we milled around a bit, wondering what to do next, then to everybody's amazement they opened the gates. That drawbridge came down!'

'Why would they do that?' said John. He looked bewildered.

Robert shrugged. 'Maybe them inside liked what we were saying.'

'So then what happened?' asked Thomas.

'We all poured inside, and before you knew it there must have been hundreds of us in there. Soldiers and servants too scared to do anything. Ha! But that Tower, the luxury inside it. I've never seen anything like it. I even went into the king's mother's bedroom. Me and my mates bounced up and down on her bed while she cowered in the corner. We wouldn't harm her – it's not her fault her son is advised by such greedy charlatans.

'I was wondering what I could get away with stealing when this great hue and cry went up. They'd found Hales and Sudbury hiding in the chapel. Well, God wasn't going to save their necks, that's for sure. They dragged them both out and took them to the execution block. That Sudbury, it took eight blows to sever his great, fat neck.

'I almost felt sorry for him,' continued Robert, although he was laughing when he said it. 'But the other one, Hales, he died quick enough. Then they put their heads on poles and they've been parading round London to show everyone what happens to the snakes that rule our country.'

Tilda was reeling. Catherine had said the world had been turned upside down. And here she was, right in the middle of a world gone completely mad. She could only hope something good would come out of it in the end.

'Where are you going now?' said John.

'Off with the mob,' Robert replied. 'I've not had so much fun since I was in the army.'

They walked on, shaking their heads. 'This is getting really out of hand,' said Thomas.

'I don't have any sympathy for Hales and Sudbury though,' said John. 'They've taxed us all half to death over the last few years.'

Back at the house, Alice was relieved to see them, but she had news herself. 'It's all over town,' she said. 'Richard has agreed to the rebels' demands. End of serfdom, people can sell the food they produce, land rent down to four pennies an acre, and there's a pardon for everyone who took part in the uprising.'

'I don't believe it,' said Thomas. He was instantly suspicious.

John readily agreed. 'It's too good to be true.'

'Well, that's what the neighbours who went to Mile End told me, and now I hear they're all drifting off. Going back home. I think this is nearly over.'

'Have you heard what's happened at the Tower?' said Thomas.

Alice shook her head. She looked wide-eyed with shock when they told her. 'Well that might put quite a different spin on things,' she said.

It had been an extraordinary day. Now it seemed everything was hanging by a thread. Thomas seemed pleased with how it had all gone, but Tilda went to bed that night wrapped with unease for the day ahead.

CHAPTER NINETEEN

June 15, 1381

Guy de Clare blinked back his exhaustion and ventured out into the street. He did not stray further than the doorway of the Franciscan monastery at Greyfriars. For now, London was quiet and the sound of the church clock at St Nicholas drifted over the still night air. Three o'clock. It would be a while yet before he would be able to take to his bed. The news from the Tower had been deeply disturbing. Hales and Sudbury executed like common criminals. Others of the court also murdered. Richard had taken it all in with his usual detachment. Guy was surprised he had stayed so calm.

Now, he could not believe the job he had been given. Two years ago he was a boy, playing blind man's buff with his brothers and sisters on the family estate back home in Gloucestershire. Today, here he was, tasked with recording the very essence of history.

While Richard and his court had taken up residence in 'the Wardrobe' in Blackfriars, he had been despatched, along with a rather intimidating lawyer whom he recognised but did not know, to oversee the production of charters of freedom and pardons for the rebels. The lawyer had worked on Guy's own written accounts – turning the demands and the promised pardons into official royal documents. Then they had been sent with an armed guard to Greyfriars and the monks there had been given the task of producing many exact duplicates of these charters and pardons – all by dawn.

Guy had been surprised to see Richard was prepared to go ahead with these concessions after hearing about what had happened at the Tower. But here they all were, squinting under candlelight to produce the documents. Documents based on the very words Guy had recorded! He had never been so frightened in his life, these last few days, but now, with the dangerous moments receding into the past, he had never felt so important. So grown-up. What a story to tell his family back home. How his father would be proud of him.

*

Tilda Rolfe woke later that morning to bright sunlight streaming through the window slats up in the attic. She could sense the heat of the day in the room and watched, half asleep, as specks of dust danced lazily in the beams. She loved Uncle John's house. He had a sturdy slate roof rather than a leaky thatch. And an 'upstairs'. It seemed like luxury compared to their peasant hut with its single room and mud floor. And outside John's front door, she had quickly realised, there was a world of great excitement and possibility. At least there usually was, when people weren't killing their neighbours out in the street and marching around with heads on poles. And even the smell of the city, which had unnerved her when she had first arrived, even that was something she was getting used to. Tilda never felt excited about living in Aylesford. Outside their door there was a cow and a horse. And a big puddle...

It had been a strange and frightening few days. But now, perhaps something extraordinary had happened. The whole world was balancing on a great wheel and it was slowly turning their way. Everyone in Southwark had heard about the king's meeting with the Essex rebels. They knew about the pardon and the king agreeing to their demands. They were FREE! It was as deep and profound as the sun coming up in the morning, or the turning of the tides.

That upheaval with the Tower of London was a puzzle though. Had Richard deliberately ordered the guards to let the peasants in, so they could seize his hated advisors? Or had it all happened without him knowing? The truth was, nobody knew. They could only guess. Like they could only guess how all this would end.

But for now, she reflected, Thomas Rolfe couldn't keep the smile from his face. Last night, just before they went to bed, he had hugged Tilda tight and thanked her for her boldness. 'When we go home, we'll be able to find work that pays us well. Or that Lord Laybourne will have to dig deeper into his pockets if he wants to keep us working for him. Well done, my lovely girl. Persuading me to come up here and do this bold thing!'

'But Father, we burned down his house,' she said. 'If the lord comes back there'll be hell to pay.'

Thomas shrugged. 'The whole world has changed, Tilda. And we've been part of it! And anyway, the king has issued pardons. Even if he does come back, we will be safe and a lot happier.'

Her train of thought was interrupted. Uncle John was shouting upstairs. 'Tilda! Come for your breakfast!'

She stirred from the warmth of her temporary bedding and stumbled downstairs. John had been out and returned with a fresh loaf of bread. He looked worried though. 'Streets are full of rumours again,' he said grimly. 'Not everyone's gone home. That Wat Tyler and a good crowd of the Essex men have stayed at Mile End. They've got more demands to make, I hear. Though I don't know what else they could ask for.'

Alice was looking anxious too. 'No offence, you two,' she said to Tilda and Thomas. 'But I want everything back to normal now. I want all the country people to go home and settle down. I don't want any more burning and murder on the streets.'

John put an arm round her shoulder. 'Come now, Alice. You can't blame Tilda and Thomas for that.'

Alice busied herself in the kitchen and did not reply. Tilda went to help her rinse the breakfast plates in a bowl of water drawn from the street pump. She could sympathise with Alice. She too was wondering how all this would end and whether there would be any more trouble in these narrow, crowded streets.

CHAPTER TWENTY

Richard greeted Guy with a warm smile when he returned from the Greyfriars monastery that morning. Soldiers had been despatched to hand out the pardons and charters to the peasants, Richard told him, and now things would settle back to normal.

'You have done your job well, Guy de Clare,' said the king. 'We are impressed. You have not failed us.'

Guy smiled and tried not to look too excited. He was learning that at court it was necessary to keep your emotions hidden. It was courteous to acknowledge such royal praise of course, most suitably with a low and prolonged bow of the head, but it would not do to gush. You had to give the impression that this was entirely what you did as a matter of course. Not grin and blush, as if the prettiest girl at the tournament had just smiled winningly at you.

'You must rest,' said Richard. 'We know you have worked throughout the night.'

Guy retired to his quarters and was asleep the moment he lay down his head. He was woken seemingly moments later by a chamber boy and instructed to prepare to leave as soon as possible. Guy was too dazed to think. The light on the walls told him it was sometime in the afternoon, but he had to wait until the nearby church clock tolled two o'clock to realise exactly where he was in the day. The chamber boy had told him to accompany Richard on another excursion. It was quiet out on the street, and was judged safe enough for the king to emerge from his hiding place.

Guy immediately felt uneasy. Was this going to be another encounter with the rustics? Was there another chance that they would be hacked to pieces by a frenzied mob, or beheaded like Hales and Sudbury? Guy had heard about the seven or eight blows it had taken to dislodge Sudbury's head and the thought of it brought a sour taste to his mouth. He couldn't imagine how agonising that would be.

He was instructed to present himself in the courtyard where soldiers and court advisors were waiting on horseback for the king to emerge. Guy was provided with his own horse, and within moments Richard appeared in full kingly regalia. The great oak gates of the Wardrobe were opened and the king and his entourage trotted out into the street. But instead of turning east, back towards the rebels and Mile End, they turned west. It was all a great mystery.

The entourage continued down the Strand and past John of Gaunt's ruined palace. The flames had long since burned out, and bodies been taken away, but there were still bloodstains on the ground. Guy shuddered as they rode past. Where they were going remained a mystery but he was grateful there were few people out and about on the streets. There were a handful of catcalls from people, but mainly the king's party were ignored or met with respectful bows and averted eyes. This was more like the old days and a sure sign that things were getting back to normal.

Presently, the huge bulk of Westminster Abbey loomed above them. Guy had been here a few times and the massive size and elaborate latticed ceiling of the abbey never failed to astonish him.

Richard held up a hand to halt his entourage by the great west door. 'We have come to ask for God's guidance,' he declared. They entered the cool interior just as sunlight burst through the vast, stained-glass windows, like a sign from God. Guy could tell Richard thought so too. He smiled to all – as if to say he could feel in his bones that God was on his side.

The king led them to the shrine of the abbey's founder, Edward the Confessor. Here he knelt down to pray as his entourage watched over him from a respectful distance.

Guy watched the hunched figure of the king, and thought how small he looked. It was here Richard had come for his coronation. Guy wondered how overwhelming that grand ceremony must have been for a child so young. All at once he felt something he had never felt previously for the strange young man who ruled his life. He felt sorry for him. To have such terrible responsibility at such a tender age. No wonder he was so cold and capricious.

Guy thought he would never want that kind of worry on his shoulders. He was grateful to fate for sparing him.

He also thought of Hales and Sudbury. He had heard they had gone to the chapel in the Tower when the peasants broke in. He wondered if they were praying for mercy and deliverance shortly before they were dragged out to their gruesome deaths. Maybe God was busy with something else at that moment. Guy hoped He was listening to Richard right now.

Half an hour passed and the sun came and went, sending the Abbey into gloomy shadows whenever it disappeared behind a cloud. Guy shivered a little in the cold stone vastness of the nave and wondered what the rest of the day held. As the abbey clock chimed the half hour, Richard got to his feet and turned to his entourage. 'We shall go to meet the rebels once again. A few hundred remain and they are gathered at Smithfield.'

Outside, the warmth of the summer day took the chill from Guy's bones but not the gnawing dread in the pit of his stomach as they headed east to meet the rustics.

CHAPTER TWENTY-ONE

Thomas Rolfe was determined to go home. Tilda could see it on his face. He had convinced himself that the revolt was over and they should go back to Aylesford and begin to enjoy the benefits of their new freedoms. But Tilda's instincts told her to hold on. She was in the attic staring out on to the street when he came up to talk to her.

'My dearing, we should start our journey before too much of the day has gone,' he said.

'Father, look out of the window. There's still a lot of people from the country around.' You could spot them easily enough. As well has having weather-worn faces and shabbier clothes, very few of them were fat. In London, Tilda had seen more plump people than she had ever seen in her life.

'We spend all our days working and heaving and tilling,' said Thomas when she pointed this out. 'A lot of this lot sit on their backsides all day. That can't be good for you, can it!'

Tilda quite liked the sound of that. The more she thought about it, the more she didn't want to return to Aylesford. 'And if they're all going back today we'll never find an inn to stay in when darkness falls,' she said.

Thomas was sharp with her. 'I know what you're up to my girl,' he said. 'You like it here and you want to stay.'

Tilda was disappointed he could read her mind so easily. 'So what if I do, Father,' she said. 'What's waiting for us back home?'

Thomas looked astonished. 'Everything will be better. We'll have the chance to work for ourselves, sell our goods at market, pay less rent...'

'Do you honestly believe that's going to happen?'

Thomas stared at the floor. For a moment he looked sad. 'You always were cleverer than me, Tilda. I know that. And you're right. I don't know how much we can trust the king and his cronies. It might be a big trick to get us to go away.'

'Let's just stay here and see how things work out – at least for another day,' Tilda pleaded.

'I'll talk to John when he comes back,' said Thomas. 'Make sure he's happy with it. I don't want him or Alice to feel we're overstaying our welcome.'

John was out talking to a customer over the river in Smithfield. The man wanted another storey built on his house, he had told them earlier. It was an urgent job. His wife was expecting another baby and the house already held five children under ten.

Tilda and Thomas went downstairs to find Alice knitting at the kitchen table. 'We're planning on heading home...' said Thomas.

Alice's face lit up before he could finish what he was going to say and she immediately sprang to her feet. 'It's been a great pleasure to meet you, Thomas Rolfe,' she said. 'And you too, Tilda. What a fine, bonny girl you are.'

Faced with such a definite goodbye, Tilda could see Thomas was lost for words. 'We just wanted to wait until Uncle John comes home, to thank him too,' she said, trying to prepare Alice for the fact that they weren't going immediately.

'Oh no, you'd best be going,' said Alice. 'Make a good start before evening. I'll prepare a little food parcel for you to take with you.'

'Thank you,' said Thomas. 'We'll just go for a final look around.'

'That went well,' said Tilda as they walked towards London Bridge. 'She can't wait to get us out of the door.'

'Probably anxious that you don't bring home another Fleming,' said her father, although she could tell he was teasing her.

Thomas bought them a meat pie to share. It was piping-hot and he couldn't resist the smell. They ate standing on the Embankment, looking over the great bridge at the teeming vastness of London with its thousands of roofs and scores of steeples and towers.

'This is a funny place,' said Thomas. 'I don't know whether I like it or not.'

'I do,' said Tilda. 'It's exciting to be here. I hope we can visit again.'

Thomas nodded. Tilda sensed this was not the time to discuss this but she did wonder if she might yet be able to persuade her father to stay.

As they watched the boats and barges go by, it slowly dawned on both of them that something was afoot. A steady stream of people were heading over the bridge in a determined and excitable way.

'I'm not sure about this,' said Thomas. 'I think we ought to go before there's trouble.'

Just then they heard a cry. 'Thomas! Tilda!' John was coming off the bridge. He was out of breath. 'The king is meeting the rebels at Smithfield. There's a great crowd of them and everyone is in a state. Something is going to happen, for sure.'

'Let's go,' said Tilda. Once again, she was sure this was history in the making.

Thomas looked afraid. 'No. This is a sign for us to leave. We've escaped with our lives. There's nothing more that can be achieved here.'

John put his hand on his brother's shoulder. 'Tilda's right to want to go, Thomas.'

'Father – think of all the history we've heard about – William the Conqueror, Richard the Lionheart, the Battle of Crécy... all these great moments that people talk about for years and years – moments that last beyond a lifetime. Well, it's happening right now, in front of our eyes.'

'I agree with Tilda,' said John. 'Come on, let's head up to Smithfield.'

And so they did.

*

The late afternoon sun was still high in the sky by the time they got to the great meadow just outside the city walls at Smithfield. An abbey set on fire during the disturbances of the previous night still smouldered away.

The crowd they could see seemed quite different from the God-fearing peasants who had proclaimed their allegiance to the king at Blackheath a mere few days ago. They were altogether surlier and they bristled with weapons – some with proper military pikes and swords. Others had agricultural scythes, pitchforks and corn-flails they had brought with them from their villages. They looked like they were spoiling for a fight. But they were much smaller in number than Tilda had expected. At Mile End, she had heard, there had been tens of thousands of people. Here were maybe four hundred at most.

'But there's still plenty of flags of St George and even a Royal Standard or two,' said John.

'Maybe they captured those. Maybe they want the king to think they're on his side and this is a trap?'

'Shall we go and join them?' said Tilda.

'No, hold back,' said Thomas. 'If this turns nasty I want to make sure we can get away easily enough.'

Tilda thought they were letting the rebels down and should go and stand with them, but this was not the time to argue with her father. Besides, a part of her didn't want any of them to risk their lives again. They had been so near to death several times since they had arrived in London. They were not cats with nine lives. They would watch from the sidelines, close to the edge of the city and its alleyways, where they could escape if need be.

It was an extraordinary scene – all these rebels waiting for something to happen. Tilda had heard soldiers talk about battle and the awful tension of the wait before the killing started. She had always been grateful, when hearing about this, that she had been born a girl. It sounded terrifying. Yet here she was now. Close enough to see this very thing. She felt excited being able to witness it, and yet ashamed of her excitement. Wouldn't it be nobler to be there with them?

'Look, there's Wat Tyler,' said Thomas. Tilda looked to where he pointed, and sure enough the barrel-chested soldier who had spoken to them back in Aylesbury was there at the front of his men, clear to see in a red tunic with black sleeves. He looked full of spit and vinegar with an insolent swagger. 'I'd say that man has been drinking,' Thomas added.

Close by, someone was holding the reins of an impressive grey horse. 'Let's hope he can stay in the saddle,' said John.

Despite their numbers, the crowd were not boisterous. They sensed death was near and this could be their final day. Instead, there was a strange weight hanging above them – a shuffling and a murmuring and a palpable air of tension.

In the distance, a soft rumble of hooves reached their ears. It was coming from the city, to be sure, not to the side or behind the rebel phalanx. It did not look like an attempt to outflank them.

An eerie stillness descended on Wat Tyler and his men. This was the moment everyone had been waiting for. The sound of hooves grew louder. Clearly the king was coming with a large number of mounted soldiers. All eyes turned to the outskirts of the city, and shortly after the king and his soldiers emerged from one of the wider thoroughfares.

Once again, Tilda felt strangely thrilled to see the king. Richard was there at the vanguard of his men. He presented an easy target for any archer or crossbowman in the rebel ranks. Just as when she spotted him at Greenwich, she thought he looked unlike anyone she had ever seen before, resplendent in a great cloak so sumptuous she struggled to even name the colour. It was a blue so deep and rich it was almost purple, and topped with a wide collar of pure white ermine. As if this was not enough to mark him out as the monarch, atop his blond curling hair, his gold crown gleamed in the sunshine. He was so astonishing to look at, it took Tilda a while to notice his horse – a great chestnut-brown charger almost as regal as its rider. She thought of Brownie, their ploughing horse, and wondered with a pang of regret whether she would ever see him again.

The king led his soldiers far enough into the field to allow them to disperse behind him. There were maybe two hundred men in all, mostly on horseback and mostly armed with the spears and swords of professional soldiers.

'Well, it looks like we have twice as many men as them,' said Thomas. 'Maybe four hundred to the king's two hundred?'

'Yes, but they're proper soldiers,' said John. 'They're used to fighting. And they're covered in armour. I still wouldn't fancy Tyler's chances if this comes to blows.'

Close by King Richard were men whose clothes suggested both wealth and influence. 'That's Sir William Walworth,' said John. 'I recognise him. He's the Lord Mayor of London. Nasty snake of a man.'

Tilda noticed a youth standing near the king. He looked so like Richard she wondered if the king had a twin. Even from a distance she could tell he was frightened but trying his hardest not to show it. He had a pen and parchment poised on a pallet. A difficult thing to do on a horse. He was about her age, she guessed. Watching history, and recording it for the future.

CHAPTER TWENTY-TWO

As the two sides faced each other, Guy de Clare regarded the rebel army with trepidation. They were outnumbered two to one, he guessed. Maybe they were a hundred yards apart. It was a distance a cantering horse could cover in a matter of seconds and certainly close enough for any archer to launch an arrow straight at the king, and at him for that matter.

Scrutinising the rebels he noticed a lot of them were carrying bows and arrows and some had crossbows. Perhaps they had looted the armoury at the Tower? Either way, this was not an encounter they were going to win by force of arms. He looked over to Richard, who was looking every inch the king in his royal finery. He was giving nothing away. He seemed as calm as ever.

From out of the mob, a rider emerged, approaching on a fine grey horse. He looked like a soldier, although he was wearing a bright red tunic with black sleeves. 'Behold Wat Tyler, the demon-in-chief,' said Richard under his breath.

Guy too guessed this man was the leader of the revolt. He seemed quite content to approach them, although a handful of other men on horseback were emerging from the mob. They had good reason to feel safe. If they were cut down by the king's men, a hail of arrows from the peasants would devastate the royal guard.

Guy watched closely. The nearer the man came, the more repellent he seemed. He had a smug, insolent look on his face and something of the appearance of a bar-room bully. William Walworth could not contain himself. 'Give me the word, Your Majesty, and I will cut down this insolent dog.'

Richard said nothing, but a small wave of the hand indicated that the lord mayor should remain where he was.

Now the upstart was there in front of them, almost close enough to strike down with a sword. The others who had come with him stayed a few yards further behind.

He regarded the king and his entourage with cold, scheming eyes. 'My lords,' he said, doing nothing to hide the mockery in his voice. 'Your Majesty.' He nodded his head, almost imperceptibly – the most they were going to get in any display of deference. 'I have a list of demands for you to agree to. And then we will all go back to our villages.'

The voice was common, vulgar. And, Guy noted with a mixture of contempt and alarm, a little slurred by drink.

'We demand our freedom,' said the man, with a broad wave of his arm. 'We demand the abolition of the aristocracy. All 'cept the king. We are loyal to Your Majesty, still.'

There was something enragingly insolent in his manner. The way he smirked as if this was all a private joke. Most threatening of all, as he spoke, the man started to toss a dagger from hand to hand. He paused a moment, expecting a response, the dagger momentarily stilled. Richard said nothing but indicated with a wave of his hand that this leader of the villeins should continue.

'We demand the abolition of the senior clergy – all except our own great churchman John Ball. He shall be the next Archbishop of Canterbury.'

The king looked puzzled. One of his courtiers whispered in his ear to remind him. 'A vexatious priest, Your Majesty. He has been preaching treason these last few months.'

'The courts and the enforcers of the law shall be run by the people themselves,' Tyler continued. 'And our final demand is this. The wealth of the bishops and the lords shall be divided among the common people.'

There was a strange silence, and a terrible, unbearable suspense. Guy wondered what on earth was going to happen next. This man continued to toss the dagger he carried from hand to hand. It was so quiet you could hear it slapping from one palm to another.

At last, Richard spoke. 'We agree to all your demands,' he said, much to the visible astonishment of his own advisors.

The rebel leader looked amazed. He seemed lost for words. 'Bring me water,' he demanded of the royal entourage. A squire trotted over on his horse and passed him a small water container. The man swilled the water around his mouth and spat it out on the ground. It was such a gesture of utter contempt that Guy could sense everyone tensing around him.

'Now bring me beer,' said the man. Another container was offered to him and he drank greedily.

Guy waited, trying to control the growing horror he felt in his gut. What would the man do next, demand that the king give him his crown?

One of Richard's advisors, somewhere behind Guy, suddenly shouted, 'I know you. You're the biggest thief in Kent.'

This shocked the rebel leader. He stared at his challenger, his face growing red with anger. Turning to his own men he called out, 'Strike his head from his body.'

But no one moved.

*

Over at the side of the field, Tilda sensed this was the moment everything would change. They had been straining to hear what was happening but they were too far away. But Tyler's order to strike the king's advisor floated loud and clear over the distance between them. When no one did so, Tilda felt her hope for the future drain away like spilt milk. Perhaps their ingrained fear of royal authority, or awe for the king, prevented them from acting on Tyler's orders? Clearly this was one drastic step no one was prepared to take.

Someone moved out from the king's entourage. 'That's Walworth,' said John. 'That's the man who is Lord Mayor of London.'

Tilda watched in trepidation as Walworth began to scuffle with Tyler, who reached for his dagger and tried to stab the lord mayor. But the blow did not penetrate his armour. Walworth reached for his own dagger and stabbed Tyler in the neck. Another one of the king's men hit him with a sword.

Tyler managed to stay on his horse. He turned around and began to ride back towards his own lines. But halfway between the two he fell from his horse, landing with a dramatic clump on the ground.

Other men with him did not stop to pick him up. After being so bold, it now seemed as if everyone had lost their nerve.

The rebels tensed, ready to fight. Tilda could see the bowmen among them readying themselves to unleash a hail of arrows on the king and his soldiers.

'Get ready to run,' said Thomas. Tilda felt sick with fear. She wondered if they too would fall victim to the hail of arrows that would soon darken the sky.

But then something extraordinary happened. King Richard broke away from his advisors and rode forward alone on his horse, straight up to the rebel lines. Tilda watched, eyes wide in astonishment. Was she going to witness the death of the King of England? But no one unleashed their arrows. They all strained to hear what he would say.

Richard spoke in a loud, clear voice. 'I shall be your captain,' he said. 'Follow me to Clerkenwell.'

'He's had it,' said John. 'They're going to kill him.'

Tilda held her breath. But her uncle John was wrong. All the bowmen loosed the tension on their bows. Arrows were returned to quivers. Richard turned his horse towards Clerkenwell, a nearby district on the northern edge of the city. The rebels all followed along behind him.

Tilda looked at the fallen body of Wat Tyler. He was trying to stand up, although even from a distance they could see he was covered in blood. Some of his men had rushed out now and helped him to his feet. They dragged him away, against the flow of the others, no doubt in search of a hospital to try to save his life.

*

Guy de Clare watched all this with astonishment. Who would have thought that Richard could be so brave? If he was like this at fourteen, what would he be like as a grown man? Clearly, he was destined to be one of England's greatest kings. All at once the king's closest advisors spurred their horses and hurried to be with Richard at the head of the column. Guy, feeling like he was in a dream, rode alongside them.

The king turned to Sir William Walworth. 'Find that verminous wretch you stabbed and finish the job.' Walworth took off in the opposite direction with two soldiers.

*

The streets closed in around them and a strange calm settled after these bizarre events. As they approached Clerkenwell, Guy heard a small group of riders approaching them from a side street. Richard's soldiers drew their swords but when the riders came into view they saw at once they were loyal soldiers. One carried a head on a spike. They held it high to show the world. It was the man who had presented the demands. The one that Sir William Walworth had stabbed in the neck.

A gasp went up from the column of peasants behind them. Guy wondered if this was another moment when they were all going to be killed? But there was something different in that gasp. It was the sound of fear rather than defiance. He knew at once that the insolent spirit that had prompted this rebellion had finally been crushed.

All around them came more soldiers. They were being mustered from across London. The more soldiers that arrived, the safer Guy began to feel. The rebels were packed into a small square now, their defiance completely gone. Most were on their knees, pleading for mercy. Richard had a look of utter triumph about him. Guy looked at the cringing rustics and realised with a guilty pleasure that he wanted to kick them all in the face. But he checked himself. He felt a fierce elation. They had won, and he was still alive.

CHAPTER TWENTY-THREE

Tilda and her father and uncle watched the rebels marching off with foreboding.

'How did that happen?' said John.

'They could have killed the king and all of his party,' said Thomas.

Tilda was too astonished to speak.

'Come on, let's hasten away before anyone comes to round us up too,' said John.

They began to walk back to Southwark. No one spoke until they reached the road close to the bridge, when Tilda said, 'If we'd stayed with the rebels we'd have had to march away with them too. Do you think they're going to kill them all?'

'We'll never know,' said John. 'I think we've had a lucky escape.'

A soldier rode up to them, a sword in his hand. Tilda feared for her life but he stopped before he got to them. 'You rustics,' he commanded. 'Go with your brothers and sisters to Clerkenwell.'

John spoke boldly. 'We are Londoners, sir,' he said confidently. 'We are not peasants. We're returning home to Southwark.'

The soldier was not going to argue. 'Be on your way,' he commanded. They didn't need telling twice.

When they reached the Rolfe household in Southwark, Alice was indignant. 'There you all are,' she scolded. 'Thomas and Tilda told me they were going back to Aylsford. But that was three or four hours ago. It's too late to go now.'

John spoke firmly. 'It's too late all round, I think.'

They told Alice what had happened. The indignation slowly left her face. 'Then of course you must stay here for a while. See what happens. If you go back to your village, they might hang you.'

Tilda was so grateful Alice had said that, and she understood the situation. It would be really difficult staying with the Southwark Rolfes if Alice resented them being there. William, Simon and Joan came into the kitchen.

'Uncle Thomas and Cousin Tilda are staying with us for a while,' said Alice. The children's faces lit up. They liked their visitors.

Tilda felt light-headed with relief for herself, but full of concern for the other rebels. What about the ones who had no London family? Were they going to be killed right then, in Clerkenwell? And if not, what was going to happen to them?

CHAPTER TWENTY-FOUR

Richard returned to Blackfriars with his advisors. Guy could sense a change in him. Had God come to his rescue following the prayers they had said that afternoon at Westminster? The king seemed at least three inches taller.

The rebels had been instructed on pain of death to return home to their villages. Guy was surprised the soldiers did not kill them then and there. But he could see the logic in not doing so. The king's guard were still outnumbered and there was a small chance that the rebels might rediscover their fighting spirit and a battle would break out on the edge of the city. Freeing the capital of this treasonous infestation was the first priority. Richard's good sense had not deserted him.

When they were back behind locked and guarded doors, King Richard turned to Guy and declared with conviction, 'Those who seek equality with lords are not worthy to live... serfs they are and serfs they still are. They will remain in bondage not as before but incomparably harsher. For as long as we live and rule by God's grace over this kingdom we shall use our sense, our strength and our property to suppress them, so that their slavery shall be an example to posterity.

'I would like you to record those words,' he said to Guy. 'I shall make a declaration about this uprising, and that is what I intend to say.'

Guy reached for a pen and parchment and tried to remember Richard's speech. He thought about how much he would have liked to kick those peasants, begging for their lives at Clerkenwell, and all at once he felt both shame and pity. What was coming was going to be horrible. He thought of Jack and Sam, the peasant boys he had played with as a child. They would have been on that march if they had lived in Kent or Essex. He was sure of it.

But he hid his feelings. The king must never know he had sympathy for these serfs.

When he has finished scribbling Richard added, 'We shall keep the peace according to the law, or by any other methods, by beheading and the mutilation of limbs.'

Guy scribbled down his words, anxious not to miss a single syllable. Richard waited until he had finished writing and continued, 'When the rabble have dispersed from London and settled back in their homes, we shall raise an army and hunt down the ringleaders. We shall have them hanged from the trees on their village greens. And the most prominent among them shall be hanged, drawn and quartered. And we shall start with that wretch John Ball – the one they had the effrontery to tell me should be Archbishop of Canterbury. I shall attend his execution myself.'

*

'What are we to do, Tilda?' said Thomas. They had left the Rolfes' house to walk again by the river. 'Do you believe what the king promised? Because I don't believe a word of it. Especially after what we've just seen.'

Rumours had been flowing thick and fast between Londoners who had come out to support the rebels when they arrived in the city. Everyone had now heard that Wat Tyler's head had been cut off and placed on a spike. And that the remaining rebels had been driven out of London with their tails between their legs.

Tilda chose her words carefully. This was her opportunity to convince her father to stay.

'Tyler's head on a spike tells me all I need to know about what's happened to the rebellion,' she said. 'They lied to us, to get everyone to go home, like you said before.'

'And what d'you think will happen to us, if we leave?' said Thomas.

'I think they will hang us,' said Tilda. 'I think Lord Laybourne will be keen to make an example of any of his tenants who abandoned their duties to march to London.' She fought back tears. 'Especially after what we did to his manor house. I think this has ended very badly.

'But I also think we have left behind a life that had no promise for us.' She grabbed her father's arm. 'We must get used to living here. There's so much we can do to make our lives more interesting, maybe even prosper.'

'But we will be taking a terrible risk, my dearing,' said Thomas. 'I don't want us to end up like those beggars and starving urchins we saw when we first arrived. And living in the wretched hovels we passed on the edge of the city. I'm sure you're right about going back to Aylesford but we face destitution here. We can't stay with John and Alice forever.'

'Father, I have a surprise for you,' said Tilda. She delved into the folds of her skirt and unpicked a loose stitch. She held out a handful of Lady Laybourne's colourful earrings – the ones she had stolen when the Aylesford manor house had been ransacked.

'Tilda, where on earth did these come from?'

She told him. 'I kept them secret, Father. I knew we were not supposed to steal from the manor – only destroy it. But I could not see these jewels melting in the flames.'

Thomas was speechless.

'I kept it to myself, in case you were angry with me,' she said.

Thomas put an arm around her. 'Tilda, I think you may have saved us. And I have an idea. We will give a pair to John. He may want to give them to his Alice or sell them. Either way, it will make Alice feel generous towards us. And he will surely know someone we can sell our earrings to. A wealthy merchant who might gladly buy them for his own wife. This will suit John and Alice well. And if we sell wisely then we should be able to find ourselves a nice little house to rent soon enough. Lovely as it is, that house is very crowded with us there too...'

*

That evening, as they sat round the kitchen table eating their supper, Thomas asked John and Alice if he and Tilda could talk with them privately, so the children were dispatched to the yard to beat a rug.

Thomas spoke with a quiet urgency. 'My brother John, Alice.' He smiled. 'You have been very kind to us. And we have taken full advantage of that kindness. But please hear me out because Tilda and I have a plan, which I hope will suit us all.

'We have realised that a return to Aylesford would be an unhappy and possibly fatal decision.

But do not fear, we will not be expecting to stay with you – at least not for much longer.' Alice's eyes narrowed. Tilda was anxious to see how she would take this news. 'But we have a plan, which I am hoping you will help us with.'

John and Alice both looked uncertain. Tilda interrupted. 'Show them, Father. Show them!' she said.

'Hush, child,' said Thomas. He delved into his pockets and brought out the earrings. 'My clever daughter picked these up on our way up to London.'

Alice's eyes widened. 'They're worth a fortune,' she said. 'We won't ask where you got them from.' His brother nodded in agreement.

Thomas continued. 'We want to give one pair to you – to keep or to sell – for your kindness. And we want to sell the other two. That will give us enough money to find somewhere to rent while we look for work. And we shall no longer need to crowd you out of your own house.'

John hugged them both. 'I know people who would be pleased to buy these from you,' he said. 'Merchants I build for. They've got that sort of money. And this kind of jewellery won't look out of place if their wives choose to wear it. And Alice and I will have to discuss among ourselves whether to keep these you have given us. Thank you.'

Alice hugged them too. She seemed relieved. And Thomas and Tilda began to feel that everything was going to work out well for them.

*

The next morning over breakfast, John had a proposal for Thomas. 'There's a lot of work out there for me – especially after the upheaval of the last few days. I'll need an extra pair of hands and I would be very happy if you would help me. It's a whole new trade, but I am sure you will be able to learn the skills you'll need.' He turned to Tilda. 'And you will have to find a job too. I'm sure there's work here for a bright girl like you.'

'Catherine has promised she will teach me to read,' said Tilda. She felt really excited about this. 'And I, in turn, can help her to speak better English.'

They spent the day looking at a couple of houses John knew about, where there were rooms to rent. There were two more to look at tomorrow. That evening Tilda went out alone to stand by the bridge to watch the sun sink in the west.

Across the river, the London skyline looked as bewilderingly busy as ever. She could still not believe how so many people managed to live so close to each other. The evening air carried a hint of the night to come, and a thousand chimneys trailed smoke up to the darkening sky.

Tilda felt gloriously excited and alive. There was nothing at all she missed about Aylesford, apart from her pet squirrel and Brownie. She did love that horse. But here in London she could learn a new trade. She could do something with her hands and her brain rather than the sweat of her brow. And maybe there was a boy out there for her... someone she could love and who would love her too.

CHAPTER TWENTY-FIVE

Autumn 1381

Guy watched the goings-on at court with an increasingly weary cynicism. The revolt had affected Richard in a way that could not be said to be desirable. It was true that the king had acted with courage and cunning. Remarkable, in fact, for a boy of tender years, Guy had heard people say. But Richard was now behaving in a way that would only make people resent him – even turn against him.

And he had been true to his word. Every week, fresh news of reprisals and executions reached the court. There had been rebellious outbreaks far and wide across the kingdom, from Gloucester to York. All had been ruthlessly suppressed. Ignoring something like that and hoping it would fizzle out, as they had done in June, had been a terrible mistake.

The lords of the manor had followed the king's instructions with great relish. The trees on every village green in Kent and Essex now held the dangling, rotting bodies of the traitor rustics who had dared to rise up against their king. It was easy enough to find them. Soldiers would arrive at a village and tell the filthy villeins they would spare their lives if they pointed out the traitors who had led their rebellion. There had been battles too – small ones, but still outright warfare. They had killed five hundred rustics at Billericay, Guy had heard.

John Ball had been hanged, drawn and quartered, as the king had ordered. Guy had never before witnessed this barbarous method of execution. It had taken every sinew in his body not to spew out his dinner as he watched at the king's side as Ball was executed at St Albans, two days after his arrest and trial. Guy had felt a shudder of revulsion as Richard, looking on with shiny-eyed glee, relished every moment. The citizens of London could see John Ball's head every day now. It was displayed very prominently on the gatehouse at London Bridge.

Guy wondered whether this unforgiving cruelty would work its purpose and supposed it would. Fear kept these rustics in their place and only plentiful application of it would save the realm from another rebellion. He could see the logic in that.

But whether the king's cruel character was right for the court was another matter. Guy had seen how quickly Richard had squandered the admiration he had earned during the revolt with his high-handed arrogance. Now, following a banquet, Richard would require the greatest magnates of the land to stand before him in silence in the throne room. He would survey them all with a jaundiced eye and when his gaze alighted on anyone, lord or lady, duke or earl, then that man or woman would have to kneel and proclaim their loyalty to the young king. Guy knew people well enough to understand such behaviour was bound to end in tragedy.

Historical Note

Although it took place over six hundred years ago, there is much about this story which remains strangely familiar, not least the city of London itself. Although London now has thirty-five bridges, rather than just the one, many of the streets, churches and districts mentioned here will be familiar to anyone who knows the capital.

Although the revolt was put down in June 1381, other revolts flared up that summer, from the north of England to East Anglia and the west country. These were quickly suppressed by soldiers loyal to the king and altogether it is thought that around 1,500 rebels were executed or died in battle. Richard's pardons and promises, made to the rebels at Mile End and Smithfield, were completely worthless.

However, the poll tax that had done so much to feed the rebels' anger was dropped and the expensive and unsuccessful war in France, which had prompted the tax, was gradually abandoned.

The serfs returned to their villages, but in the long run the feudal system was doomed. Without an expensive and official police force it became impossible for local lords to maintain a productive labour force with their mutinous, resentful peasants. In the decades to come, many peasants simply ran away from their manors in search of better-paid work. Many others bought their freedom as local lords realised that selling 'freeman' status to their villeins was a useful way to raise income. The feudal system familiar to Thomas and Tilda Rolfe had died out by 1500.

Although the uprising was a failure, it has remained an inspiration ever since, not least for those who rose up to fight the English Civil War, the Jacobite Rebellion and the American War of Independence. Further attempts to impose poll taxes – where everyone pays the same regardless of income, by leaders from Charles I in 1641 to Margaret Thatcher in 1990, have met with open rebellion and ended in failure.

Richard II's leadership during the rebellion remained the high point of his reign. The following year he married fifteen-year-old Anne of Bohemia but there were no children. The marriage was not approved by the court and Richard's arrogant personality and failure as a military leader added to his unpopularity among the most powerful figures in the land.

When his cousin Henry Bolingbroke whom he had sent into exile as a possible rival in 1398, returned to lead an army against him, he received widespread support. Richard surrendered to him, on the promise that his life be spared. Bolingbroke agreed and became King Henry IV. The deposed former king was imprisoned in the Tower of London and later moved to Pontefract Castle in Yorkshire. When Henry discovered Richard and accomplices were plotting Richard's return to the throne, he had him murdered. How this was done remains a mystery. One rumour suggests that Richard was deliberately starved to death, although this does seem an unlikely fate for someone who needed to be dispatched with a degree of urgency. He was thirty-three and had been king for twenty-three years.

Both Henry IV and Richard II are the subjects of plays by William Shakespeare. Preacher John Ball's evocative couplet *When Adam delved and Eve span, Who was then the gentleman?* remains familiar to many and still strikes a chord with anyone concerned with inequalities in the world.

9781408858516

It is July 1945, Hitler's Third Reich has fallen, and Berlin is in ruins. The war may be over, but danger lurks in the shadows of the wreckage as Otto and his friends find themselves caught between invading armies, ruthless rival gangs and a strange Nazi war criminal who stalks them...

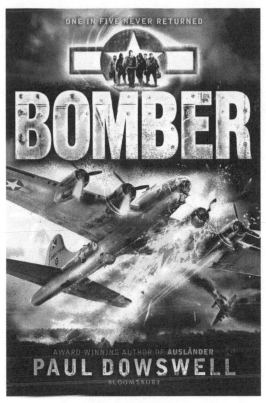

9781408858493

Harry Friedman is the gunner of the Macey May, an American Flying Fortress stationed in East Anglia. The Second World War is raging and the Nazis have swept over Europe. The crews of every Flying Fortress face terrible odds on their bombing missions. To make it through alive, Harry will need luck on his side and courage...

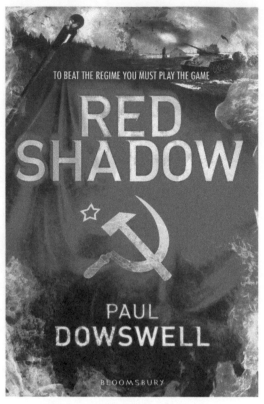

TO BEAT THE REGIME YOU MUST PLAY THE GAME

RED SHADOW

PAUL
DOWSWELL

BLOOMSBURY

9781408826249

Fifteen-year-old Misha's life is about to transform
when his father is offered a job in Stalin's inner
circle. They move into a luxurious apartment in the
Kremlin, but doubts about the glorious new Russia
quickly surface. Then, as German troops advance
on Moscow, the atmosphere in the Kremlin ignites.
Misha finds himself at the heart of a battle against
the mighty state...

9781408826232

The destinies of a German Storm Trooper, an American airman and a British Tommy converge on the final day of a global conflict. War becomes incredibly personal as nationality and geography cease to matter to each of these teenagers on the Western Front, and friendship becomes the defining aspect of their encounter. But who will live and who will die before the end of the day?

SEKTION 20

PAUL
DOWSWELL

'A heart-racing and hugely impressive thriller'
THE BOOKSELLER

9781408808634

Alex lives in East Berlin. The cold war is raging
and he and his family are forbidden to leave. But
the longer he stays the more danger he is in. His
parents start to realise that leaving the East may be
the only option left to them, but getting across the
Wall is practically impossible. And even if Alex
and his family make it to the other side, will they
be able to escape the reach of the Stasi?

9780747594192

When Peter's parents are killed, he is sent to an orphanage in Warsaw. Then German soldiers take him away to be measured and assessed. They decide that Peter valuable: with his blond hair, blue eyes, he looks just like the boy on the Hitler-Jugend poster. Someone important will want to adopt him. But Peter doesn't want to be a Nazi, and so he is going to take a very dangerous risk...

To find more historical fiction from Bloomsbury visit
www.Bloomsbury.com